Assassins Road

He heard two soft footsteps behind him. But there was a communications breakdown between his ears and his brain. He went on thinking. There was another tiny footstep like the fairy must take to get on top of the Christmas tree. His mind came awake. It was too late. Pain from the blow on his head whipped down to his heels. His knees buckled. Another blow cracked down on his head.

Then everything was splintered black chips swirling round him.

Other titles in the Walker British Mystery series:

Marian Babson • THE LORD MAYOR OF DEATH
John Creasey • HELP FROM THE BARON
Elizabeth Lemarchand • UNHAPPY RETURNS
W.J. Burley • DEATH IN WILLOW PATTERN
John Sladek • INVISIBLE GREEN
William Haggard • YESTERDAY'S ENEMY
Elizabeth Lemarchand • STEP IN THE DARK
Simon Harvester • ZION ROAD
Peter Alding • MURDER IS SUSPECTED
John Creasey • THE TOFF AND THE FALLEN ANGELS
J.G. Jeffreys • SUICIDE MOST FOUL
Simon Harvester • MOSCOW ROAD
Josephine Bell • VICTIM
John Creasey •   THE BARON AND THE UNFINISHED PORTRAIT
Jeffrey Ashford • THREE LAYERS OF GUILT
Elizabeth Lemarchand • CHANGE FOR THE WORSE
Marian Babson • DANGEROUS TO KNOW
William Haggard • VISA TO LIMBO
Desmond Cory • THE NIGHT HAWK
Jeffrey Ashford • SLOW DOWN THE WORLD

SIMON HARVESTER
Assassins Road

WALKER AND COMPANY · NEW YORK

Copyright © 1965 by Simon Harvester

All rights reserved. No part of this book may be reproduced or transmitted in any form or by any means, electric or mechanical, including photocopying, recording, or by any information storage and retrieval system, without permission in writing from the Publisher.

All the characters and events portrayed in this story are fictitious.

First published in the United States of America in 1965 by the Walker Publishing Company, Inc.

This paperback edition first published in 1983.

ISBN: 0-8027-3014-0

Library of Congress Catalog Card Number: 65-23645

Printed in the United States of America

10 9 8 7 6 5 4 3 2 1

For

GILES POMFRET

Dear Giles:
It seems nearer in experience than it is in time that we were indulging our twenty-year-old inclinations by scrambling around Cairo and the Pyramids. Great days. Do you remember . . . no, this is not the occasion.

Since then I have been fortunate to have your advice and suggestions on matters relating to those of all persuasions in the Middle East who gave us hospitality and discussion. So here is a story for you which may revive mutual recollections. You will also find on the final pages that I have struck a blow for our attitude towards the incoherence which others have made of transliterations of Arabic into English.

SIMON

There is in the intelligence officer, whether he operates at home or abroad, a certain 'front-line' mentality, a 'first-line-of-defence' mentality. His awareness is sharpened because in his daily work he is almost continually confronted with evidence of the enemy in action. If the sense of adventure plays some role here, as it surely does, it is adventure with a large measure of concern for the public safety.

ALLEN DULLES
The Craft of Intelligence

I

THIS is a city.

It is a city in what is called, illogically, the Middle East. During these summer months you can enjoy its location best in early morning when the cupolas and manarats and spires of holy places and centres of instruction rise into the sunshine above the clusters of cypresses. At every hour it looks and smells like a very old city. It should do. It is. History encrusts every infinitesimal speck of its dust. Bloody battles galore have been fought here, some between vast armies, some between fanatical groups, some between both. It is still an unquiet city. Stop on any street corner or stand on the stony slopes of nearby hills, and listen. You can almost hear the lurking animosity like the vibrance of gathering thunder. At places you can see its visible manifestations.

Local people demonstrate praiseworthy resistance to twentieth-century fads and neuroses. The women form one distinct group. Old brown-skinned women shapeless in rusty black robes which cover them from head to foot. Barefoot little girls in grubby floral dresses playing hide-and-seek around big shiny cars or groups of dun-coloured buses. Comely women wearing long white head-shawls and ankle-length black dresses whose corsage is embroidered with vari-coloured panels of needlework flowers, stately as queens under the wide heavy baskets balanced on their heads. One thing about them strikes you at once: the resigned patience of their eyes and lips. They come from unimportant back streets. Then there are priests, men who wear different types of habit. And there are the indigenous men, natives of this city and the surrounding countryside.

Some people say you can guess something or know it or imagine it but you cannot 'sense' it. That is wrong here. You sense the essential difference of these men. There are Arabs in red-and-white chequered *qeffiyahs* and robes with ingrained shadows of desert dust. There are city Arabs with plump cheeks and darting quick eyes, clad in their one Western-style, greasy jacket and trousers, making a living from their wits. There are soldiers. And traders from *suqs* who resemble biblical prophets. There are whitebearded *mullahs* more familiar with ancient turmoils than they are with events of their own age. There are Jewish elders whose heads are so full of Old Testament dramas that today's news is flat beer for them. What differentiates these men from others is their eyes. You sense that they believe they live on the verge of some gigantic manifestation of divine intervention. Among the young and middleaged the eyes are hot and brooding; among the old they are contemplative and brooding. You sense that they believe themselves animated by realities unfelt by men elsewhere, as if each one regarded himself as a part of legend.

You sense this difference. No other word describes accurately your reaction because nothing gives reason for what you feel yet it goes deeper than imagination. Your nerves and blood respond to it. It is part of the unheard thunder. Some old cities have that effect on their native sons. And this is an old city. The central focus of architecture amid the hillsides has scarcely changed during hundreds of years.

So there are old men who aspire to wisdom and young ones hopeful of enforcing their beliefs. There are priests deep in their faiths and dogmas. Some men would sell your life faster than they could swat a fly. They would prefer to kill you with a knife; it is quieter. Others will attribute whatever happens to you, from poverty and persecution to preventable disease and enormous wealth, to the will of God. Perhaps it is; can you prove it is not? Confidence men peddle 'holy' relics or entice your money for non-existent film companies and oilwells. There are pickpockets, lunatics, fanatics, and men and women possessed by spirits and devils.

If you go out after dark to get the night feel of the city the patient-eyed women have gone. In their place are whores. Now it's strange they should be here because this city is stricter about the morality of women than it is about assassination and murder. But they are here, as they are in every city, though they are thrown out directly they are caught, but until then they lurk about, trying to ward off poverty or give vent to an aspect of their nature which the doctors may subdue one day. They are young and thin, lithe and tempestuous, and have heavy-lidded dark eyes which seem older than those of the wise men. Some have acquired an incongruous smatter of primitive foreign words which are spoken as they emerge from patchwork shadows and retreat into them to await another lone tourist.

It spreads around you, an old Middle East city with history under every stride, a history of good and evil, courage and cowardice, treachery and saintliness, intolerance and wisdom and resignation, folly and savagery, though nobody looking up at its night-shrouded walls and seeing starlight illuminate sandbags on their dim parapets would say that the hopes which this city enshrine have been realized. They have not. Cities are cities. People are people. And this is not a peaceful city. It is a holy city. Christians venerate it, Jews associate their kings and prophets with it, Muslims say that Mahomet ascended from it to Heaven. An old old city. Its name is Jerusalem.

Dorian Silk held his breath. On this hot summer night he was getting adept at it. In the last forty minutes, standing motionless among shadows near the Dung Gate, he had kept doing it. His lungs felt like outsize football bladders inflated to bursting point. He was sure the exercise did him a power of harm. The other man went past at a soft-shoed shuffle.

When the night went quiet again Silk let out his breath. His thoughts returned to Jerusalem and what he was doing here.

They did not make him wildly happy or serenely content. He disliked cities. Unlike other men, he felt no glow of achievement from saying he had lived in or visited this or that well-known squash of streets, paid its inflated prices for everything, seen its temporarily famous figures turn their benign gaze on smirky bootlickers smelling just that rank under kindlier names, let its restaurants and waiters rook him, endured its traffic frustrations, inhaled its cancer-laden fumes, put up with its buck-passers and status-symbol worshippers and other members of the smirk brigade, and witnessed its headlong rush to tomorrows which were coming anyway. If you took pride from that you should sell your head, brother, not just leave it in pawn. The market price for solid brass was dicey.

He held his breath again. The *bint* loitered wearily past, less than ten yards off, shapeless from head to foot though the shawl over her hair would fall around her neck if she saw a potential customer. Other shadows hid her. He relaxed. No, cities lacked attraction for him. Jerusalem was somewhat different. It was a living symbol of the treachery of men.

As he stood there a slight breeze stirred towards him through darkness veiling the Valley of Kidron. Usually it brought reminders of Jordan sands and Dead Sea salt. Tonight it was empty of definite odours.

He gave his contact another ten minutes. Spies become conditioned to waiting impatiently, poised on the needle-point of each new second.

The minutes passed uneventfully. He heard only the pulse of his own blood. When the minutes ended he turned back alongside the city wall over Mount Ophel, starting to make his way to Jericho Road. After a short distance he turned north up a street leading to the Pinnacle of the Temple. His shoes made scarcely any sound on the gritty road surface.

That was fortunate. It left his ears free to pick up signals. They heard the flip-flip-flip of tiny footsteps coming up fast behind him. It might just be the scurry of a contrite husband though such a man here came under the heading of the eighth wonder of the world. And no *bint* or loving wife rushed home quietly in male shoes.

As the flip almost caught up with him, he collapsed forward. It was the most effective tactic here. He could always say he had dizzy spells at full moon. When he fell the other man was about to breathe down the back of his neck. He sagged, broke his fall with his hands, rolled over and reached out. His groping hand missed. The other man let out a gasp of jerky air and stumbled, signs which told how his body had been poised on the balls of his toes and thrown off-balance. Something tinkled metallically on the ground. It was close enough to what was admitted as the face of Silk to be unwelcome.

He writhed forward. His clutching fingers caught hold of a trouser leg. The material was thin and felt dusty. The point of a mis-aimed shoe struck the side of his head a glancing blow. He hung onto the trouser leg, wrenching it towards him. The material ripped. His action forced the other man to adjust his stance as he swung his foot round for another kick.

Silk felt the edge of the shoe scrape his eyebrows. Instantly he heaved himself forward, shoving his head and shoulders between the separated legs. Unable to maintain his balance, the other man bent at the knees and fell on his back. He fell intelligently. Silk crawled up over threshing legs. A fist struck the side of his head. It jerked away and hit him again. Both blows lacked strength. He guessed that his assailant was without another weapon and was frightened lest he be taken whole and enticed to talk. At present the other man was giving a lifelike impression of an octopus bothered by delirium tremens, arms and legs threshing while his body writhed to free itself. This heavy darkness hampered Silk, masking the rolling head. More by luck than judgment he bopped the man under the left ear. It was a wasted effort. He crawled on up the heaving body with some hope of sitting on the man's chest to wait for fatigue. Then a haymaker blow got him on the right side of the jaw. It hurt and knocked him off-balance. They rolled over and over slugging each other as best they could, wrapped in a loverly embrace. He sighed inwardly. It was just like an ancient Western movie showing off what television could achieve. He grunted as a knee dug into his belly. Then another haymaker crashed onto his jaw. The top of his head and his eyes seemed to go off through the swirling shadows. He fell onto his side. One part of his mind kept his limbs active.

When his head became one unit again he was alone. He crabbed around searching for the other man but his assailant had gone. The road, its geometric shadows, was quiet; he heard or imagined that he heard only the night snuffle of donkeys. It might be empty. Night pedestrians under the sandbagged walls of this divided holy city were few and none lingered if they heard sounds of a scuffle. Armed patrols were suspicious of night brawlers. Modern Jerusalem, like the city which had been here long before Christ, lived on a hairline of religious tolerance.

He fumbled around while his head cleared. Eventually he found what he was seeking and dropped it into the pocket of his jacket. Keeping to shadows he crept to the nearest wall and stood up. His breath came back while he looked round. If there was anyone about they were keeping their presence a closer secret than the Pharaohs had kept their treasure.

'Cowboys and Indians, cowboys and Indians,' he muttered softly, and sucked blood off the grazed knuckles of his right hand.

After a couple of minutes he resumed his walk, licking his knuckles. Almost at once a *bint* came towards him from a chessboard pattern of shadow and starlight. Her saunter gave no indication of how long she had been nearby. He went on at the same casual pace though his hands hung idle at his sides. She might be out front for somebody.

At his approach the girl halted some five or six strides off his direct line. He was unsurprised when her shawl slid off her hair.

She was just too far off for him to see her though the starlight illuminated his face clearly. That was unimportant. This dim light was calculated to recommend even Picasso's three-eyed women as raving beauties. Her shapeless dark clothes were an open invitation for lonely masculine imagination to frolic around enjoying itself. He saw large hollow-circle glinty rings hanging from her ears and a mop of tangled black hair. He guessed that she had lean cheeks and a short aquiline nose and well-shaped lips. He also guessed that she was slightly older than most *bints* who wandered out at night. The rest was pure imagination.

As he drew level he shook his head at her. Without speaking she drew back into the darker shadows and went on down the street. He heard her quiet footsteps fade into silence. A short distance farther on he put his back against a darkened wall and looked round. The girl had vanished. He heard only a snuffle of donkeys. It was quiet, too quiet. He got out his automatic and walked on.

Some forty minutes later he let himself into his hotel bedroom. He locked the door, rested his back against it for a moment, and then switched on the light. For over twelve years he had lived in Muslim countries, scarcely ever away from mosques and deserts which were home to the Faithful in Islam, and this bedroom was a carbon copy of at least fifty which he had occupied. It was small, hot, drab, and he was given a rapturous welcome home by legions of delighted flies. No doubt his wingless bedfellows would be similarly ecstatic when they had an opportunity to greet him as their pet fatted calf.

He loosened his tie and raised his head to listen. The man in the room on his left was praying again in his loud deep voice. In the room on the other side the fat young couple were about halfway through the nightly argument which preceded happier domestic sounds. Overhead a radio raved the 'Voice of the Arab' from Cairo. And somewhere the plumbing gurgled like an old camel. It never ceased. At night its belches had a triumphant supremacy over other noises.

Yawning, he went across and sat down on the Victorian brass bedstead which gave an appearance of having witnessed much sin. Even the spreading blotches of discolouration on the brass resembled the evidence of nameless diseases. He bent forward wearily to take off his shoes and socks, and wiggled his aching toes. His feet were in rebellion from wandering round Jerusalem for an average ten hours a day since he got here nearly two weeks ago. Yawning again, he straightened his back, stretched his arms, and wished the mystic next door could try to claim his Maker's attention with a quieter voice. He fished out the knife dropped by his assailant.

It was about twelve inches long, pointed, the seven-inch blade razor-sharp on each side. Blade and handle were separated by a poor quality steel bar of about six inches from end to end and half an inch wide. The manufacturers were bashful about their responsibility. He cleaned his nails delicately with the tip of the blade.

He grunted up onto his feet and padded across the faded carpet to the plain chest-of-drawers beside the window. As usual the top left-hand drawer stuck. At the fourth attempt he yanked it open. He shoved aside two almost clean shirts, some unripe socks, and lifted out the knife underneath. It was the same length but its blade had only one cutting edge and its handle was bound in cheap yellow wire.

He studied the knives thoughtfully. Two nights ago he

had taken the other knife from a man of heavier build and slightly taller after a shorter rumpus at approximately the same place. It was getting monotonous. He laid them down and sucked his grazed knuckles. Then he searched around for his bottle of surgical spirit.

2

'First, one vital point,' Silk said and interrupted himself. 'Oh yes, thanks for coming. Very civil of you. I do need help, hence my cable. Now about this vital matter, your recent and doubtless directed suggestion that I should have a cosy holiday at home and then assist counter-espionage. No.'

It was two days later. Afternoon heat made the room as sweetly fresh as a feather-bed long enjoyed by an unwashed beefy man and his buxom wife. Even the flies drowsed while they did their helicopter hover.

Swann perched on Silk's bed. He was bent forward to straighten the saffron clocks on his lilac silk socks. They did not complement his mustard-hued shoes and immaculate white suit but they pleased him. So presumably did his blue-striped, squashed strawberry cotton shirt and large mauve butterfly bow tie with its polka dots which shone bronze from one angle and neon green from another. Swann invariably scattered raw colours over himself like an infection. People stared at him disbelievingly. Nobody was likely to take him for an intelligence officer. He looked atrocious.

When his socks were straight he sat up. He looked thinner than ever. The kinky grey hair floating above his tiny ears resembled torn cobwebs. His pale eyes blinked through plain glass spectacles.

'Why not?' he asked cautiously.

'I've been home,' Silk reminded him and belched. 'I should never eat hearty at lunch. I haven't got an expense-account digestion. I went home last year. Rush rush rush. Traffic. Bad tempers. Bad manners. Rush rush rush. Status symbols and psychiatrists to prove it. And politicians. God and television, those politicians! What mice-holes did they crawl out of? Such wee men with such inflamed opinions of themselves. No, mate. No. As a patriot, I find it better to be where I can't see what is happening back there. Even the new architecture is a bloody bore. Lumps of grey sugar.'

As he went on, Swann gazed at the escalating flies as if they set a unique scientific problem.

The silence told Silk that he was being indulged. Swann made allowances for his men. He knew that espionage agents had scant respect for contemporary political careerists, the 'My friends' and 'Comrades' gaggers. He knew too that counter-espionage agents were a different breed. They were home-based. They grew a smile so hardy that beside it the chorus-girl variety was anaemic. They saw Ministers regularly and prayed over their pink gins that some Minister would ultimately see them. Silk admired politicians like he welcomed a horrible memory.

He went on talking.

Swann and Silk got on together. They had done since the days when Silk did his first Middle East job and became an absorbed student of Arab affairs and the influence of Islam from the Atlantic to the central Asian Sino-Russian frontier. Away from the theatre and a marriage lost down contemporary social plumbing, Silk had done well. Others had greater flair, charm, sagacity, other qualities. Silk had stubbornness.

Neither their cordiality nor the years of working together meant much. Agents had to rely on each other but they never trusted each other. This age included men like George Blake and Kim Philby, far removed from the trustworthy figures conjured up by Rudyard Kipling. Modern agents never went to sleep full of boyish faith. Not unless they had a compulsive death wish.

That was one comprehension shared by agents. There were others. High on Swann's personal list were women. Women terrified Swann. He never used a homosexual spy, inevitably a ripe case for blackmail, but he got nervous dyspepsia over those who were ordinary heterosexual, aware that tension and the slack hours before tension heightened the sexual appetite of many men. He thought wives were disastrous. They too were blackmail material. His views were monkish.

Working spies shared other comprehensions. Among them was one that no agent would let anyone persuade him to act the role of a disgraced man, flung out of the service and into gaol and later found lying in a gutter for a Russian agent to find. This threadbare Victorian melodrama, *A Hero Misjudged* or *His Name Besmirched*, might amuse credulous old gentlemen hankering after hansom cabs and silent skies, but it would have Russian agents tittering as they stepped over the outcast figure. It was a matter of elementary logic. If the outcast was truly a disgraced British spy, then by the day he reached the gutter every scrap of information at his disposal would be outdated, codes and ciphers altered, addresses and names changed, and the Russians would know he was useless to them. The Soviet KGB did not employ fools.

Agents whom the Powers assigned to Middle East duty shared other comprehensions. They became the most sophisticated in the game. British agents started with considerable advantages over other Western agents. They knew the Arab world.

The Middle East was a gigantic dustbin acrawl with antagonisms. By contrast, such corners of predictable espionage patterns as Berlin and southeast Asia were placid acres.

Egyptian agents were everywhere. Such was the resolution of Nassah's espionage that his agents often duplicated their work. Nests of other agents abounded: anti-Egyptian

Syrians, anti-Nassah Arabs, Jordanian extremists, self-exiled Iranian tribesmen, fellow-travellers of Peking, Ba'athist supporters, Army officers from every country who were all things to all men as they intrigued and murdered to seize power, Arab clans who fought each other, Jews fearful of the Arab attack on Israel which was being mounted as Egyptian rockets multiplied. And everywhere, creeping out of large hotels and stinking alleys alike, were men without political affiliations who sold lives and information for a few pounds to anyone. Espionage tensions were higher here than anywhere else in the world.

Consequently, Swann indulged the individual temperaments of his men. He showed particular consideration for those who seldom drank and took on the strain of working alone for months. He was father, confessor, manager, instructor, whatever the situation required.

His chief worry about Silk was a particular woman, an Afghan. He had a full dossier on her and had seen her. She was intelligent and probably attractive though he knew nothing about female attraction. Fortunately, Silk behaved sensibly. He stayed away from her.

So for innumerable reasons Swann sat on the bed watching the flies while he let Silk talk. Occasionally he raised his brows or nodded. Once he actually smiled. He knew that talk was Silk's method of loosening strains. Only agents of the American CIA would get apprehensive over his views on British politicians. Having heard him for half an hour they would emplane for Washington and its Pentagon in understandable anxiety over the morale of at least one British agent. Swann would have been suspicious if Silk had not talked as he did.

At length he interrupted. 'Well now,' he said amiably.

Silk scratched his nose. 'You won't like this,' he said candidly. 'It's a flaming insult. What do you know about the Prophet?'

'Mahomet?'

'No. A modern boy, a killer, perhaps just a label.'

'Muslim?'

'Ah, the sixtyfour billion piastre question. Who is Muslim? If they're Arabs they'll swear blind they are but they'll still get up to unMuslim activities.'

'More.'

Silk drew a dirty folded slip of notepaper from the tiny waist pocket inside his trousers and went across the room to give it to Swann. 'Take a butcher's at that,' he said.

Swann unfolded it carefully. Open, it was less than quarto size. The paper was of poor quality, semi-porous, and faintly brown. The message on it was long. The writer had written with a sharp pencil and in small neat capital letters. He held it up to the light from the window. Faint discolourations crossed the message.

'Did you test it?' he asked.

'Spencer. No known secret inks.'

'Does its clear make sense?'

'Here we go,' Silk said. He sat down on the one rickety chair and crossed his legs. 'The morning after I got it I had a go at it myself hoping to save time. At first the letter frequency threw me. Then I saw that the third most frequent letter was O and the fifth was R.'

'Spanish?'

'Ah.'

'What cipher?'

'It looked like simple substitution without frequency suppression. The O was one guide. When I reached that point I had run out of time, there was a possibility of my real mission hotting up, so I sent it to Spencer. He sent it back a week later.'

'How long ago was that?'

'Three weeks the day after tomorrow.'

Swann nodded. He avoided the questions asked by most intelligence officers, men who suffered a rush of blood directly the detested subject of codes and ciphers arose.

The worst were those like one man Silk had met who looked terribly keen and ticked off fundamentals on his fingers, beginning with 'the most commonly used letter in European languages is E with a frequency of 988 in German, 850 in French, 678 in Spanish, and 591 in English per thousand words', working his route down the alphabet just to prove he was with it. Swann let his men believe they had a grain of sense.

'Few doubled letters,' he observed.

'In sequence that was the third point which led me to believe it was Spanish. The second was that when I came by it, as they say, I was in Marraqesh and its Spanish Civil War refugee population and their families seem much higher. I found that words on two selections of lines averaged 5·21 letters. That's 0·25 above Spanish but higher than French and considerably less than German.'

'Wait. What sort of hotel were you staying at?'

'Moroccan.'

'How Moroccan?'

'No Paris chef, no Swiss waiter, no Las Vegas entertainers.'

'European guests?'

'Two. British. He and she. Good manners, pre-kitchen sink drama. Rather sweet.'

'Tourists?'

'Journalists on holiday.'

'Ages?'

'Middle thirties,' Silk said. 'I doubt if they had anything to do with the message.' He interrupted himself. 'Did you get in touch with the buggers for me?'

'What were and are you?' Swann asked as he brought out two fountain pens and laid them on the bed. Beside them he put six tie-clips, four ordinary size cigarette packets, and three match boxes. 'The buggers gave me two of their special new audit-boxes for you. They're in my brief-case.'

'I hope they work,' Silk said and examined a match box.

'I am myself, a British newsagency reporter, former travel agent. I say, the buggers are getting dead clever, aren't they? Look at this.'

'What does the clear of the message say?'

'This is where insults pile on thick and fast,' Silk said. He pulled out the old narrow leather belt which supported his trousers. He opened one concealed pocket in it, drew up a tiny folded square of ricepaper, and shook it open. He held it out. 'Read that.'

'You read it. I've got a migraine coming on.'

'Want a pill?'

'I'll have a couple later if it gets worse.'

'Right,' Silk said. 'Open your lugs. This begins by announcing that one Ibrahim ben Fasi will be killed four days after I got it. It goes on that arrangements have been completed to despatch Ahmad al Salim the next day and Shaikh Fahad Mubaraq one week later. Then there was to be a gap of three weeks followed by the rainbow sneeze of Messrs. Abdullah Sabri, Ezad Iryani, Mohsin Salama, and Yusuf ibn Murtaqi. It ends by saying that the Prophet has prepared another list of deaths which will be circulated shortly. It is signed The Prophet. Now——'

'Wait a bit, son,' Swann interrupted. 'About the first three.'

Silk put the slip of paper into his pocket and said: 'Guess.'

'How?'

'Ben Fasi, car accident near Algiers. Al Salim among sixty-odd people who vanished on a flight over the South Atlantic to Buenos Aires. Shaikh Mubaraq of a heart attack after dinner in Bahrain.'

Swann frowned at the drowsily yo-yoing flies. 'Could they have been saved?' he asked.

Silk shook his head as he refastened the belt around his waist. 'No,' he said. 'Spencer's clear reached me after the first two had left us. It took me a week to locate a likely ben Fasi. In fact I was onto al Salim first. Newspapers gave his name on the plane's flight list. A Libyan. But one al

Salim is like one Mr. Smith. Then last week I learned about Mubaraq. A Saudi Arabian.'

Swann knuckled his forehead. 'Why didn't you contact us rightaway?' he asked.

'It might have been a dodge to winkle me into the open. If I had contacted you somebody might have been waiting.'

'Why are you here when you should be some distance away on your real mission?'

'The other job has reached the lull before the storm. We thought it best to disperse briefly and regather when everything is good and ripe. I came here because Abdullah Sabri may be here.'

'Any proof?'

Silk went over to the chest-of-drawers. 'Lately,' he said, and opened one drawer. 'One of my contacts thought he knew of an Abdullah Sabri who might be the man and arranged for an unknown individual to take me to him.' He shut the drawer, turned across the room and dropped the two knives beside Swann. 'Souvenirs of my endeavours to meet the unknown individual.'

Swann tch-tched like a fretful stockbroker. 'When were you rumbled?' he asked.

'You guess.'

Swann glared at the knives. 'Of all the goddam nerve!' he exclaimed and stood up. 'My men deserve decent steel, not shoddy junk.'

'Well, thanks. Shall I give them one with a chased gold handle?'

Swann began pacing irritably round the bedroom. 'Do they know what you are?' he asked.

'Maybe, maybe not. But you'd better have a pill now. That question was in the wrong place. You haven't asked how I got the message. I went for a walk through the Qasbah in broad daylight. When I got back to my hotel it was in my pocket.'

'Ah,' Swann said fretfully. 'Have you found any locating or uniting factors?'

'My examination is sketchy. Al Salim may provide a clue. He was a minor government trade official. Ben Fasi was head of a Moroccan customs department. But Mubaraq doesn't fit the pattern. He was shaikh of a minor Saudi Arabian tribe.'

Swann might have a cracking headache but he heard the slight change in Silk's voice. 'What about Mubaraq?' he asked abruptly.

'Until recently his joys were family pride and rifles. He could only afford two wives and one concubine.'

'Now?'

'Oil under his feet.'

'Exploitable?'

'Milking cows is harder.'

After a brief hesitation Swann asked: 'What about those who are still alive?'

'Hell, give me a chance. I've followed it up while doing this other job. I can't do everything.'

'Keep your temper. Who used this junk on you?'

'No idea.'

'Pity,' Swann commented phlegmatically. 'Well, go on.'

Silk frowned. 'You know how this other job is hotting up,' he said. 'That's why I wanted to see you. We may be busy for weeks. This Prophet business seems real. I thought you might fly someone here to take over. Incidentally, since then another of my disreputable contacts has told me I may get to Sabri through a Mahmoud Amer whom I shall try to see tonight. After then it's up to you.'

'How long can you stay here?'

'Impossible to say. Five days at the outside but don't count on it. Why?'

Swann drew his thin fingertips along his forehead. 'As usual our trouble is men,' he complained. 'We're stretched to the limit. I wouldn't have loaned you to Dryden if he had enough men for this other mission. Whitehall just won't find money for our work.'

'Ah, but it'll find the stuff for kiwi planes and groundnuts which won't grow. We're surrounded by Lilliputian politicians, little squeaking men who posture, who live in terror of trade union bosses and the UN. A pox on all their houses. We need——'

'Please,' Swann interrupted. 'I've heard it once today.' He took off the futile glasses and shut his eyes, rubbing the lids. 'Do you think there is something in this Prophet business?'

'I'd go after it,' Silk said. 'That's why I'm here.' Then his anger hardened. 'It's a flaming insult. The cutlery is the least of it. But that's how they think out here. The Middle East hasn't learned anything new about human relationships for five thousand years. You'd think the Sumerians were still fighting the Akkadians. . . . about this "Prophet". If he is real, as an organisation, then when the news gets around people will say it's the rebirth of the Assassins.' He hesitated to let the point sink in; the Assassins, the model for Murder Inc. and Cosa Nostra, had done pretty well as a terrorist society operating from the hills of Iran nine hundred years ago and their influence lasted for two centuries. He knew the point was not lost on Swann; history was Swann's speciality. He said: 'It has possibilities. You arrange murders and create a record of it. Then you announce your existence. Imagine the effect on the average people of these parts.'

Swann was silent for some while. Then he opened his eyes.

'Maybe you have stumbled into something,' he said cautiously.

'Stumbled or was shoved.'

'You think the message was put into your pocket deliberately.'

'I am a reporter hunting for news.'

'Mmmm-mmh. Do you suppose this began on the Nile?'

'No.'

'Why?'

'Publicity. Cairo *biqbashis* are like a failing actress

chasing publicity through a divorce. You need oxyacetylene gear to burn the microphones free from their hands.'

'Nicely put, the ex-playwright personified, but inconclusive.'

'Oh, there is more,' Silk said. He leaned forward, elbows on knees, hands hanging limp. His face had what Swann called his Arab expression, the look which settles quietly but inexorably on the faces of men used to travelling across the great solitude of the deserts and who see the fallen ruins of great cities which prospered when these wastes were greenly wooded or only a fraction of their present size, an expression which tells how the men know themselves part of the blowing dust of history. 'On my real mission I've been in fourteen cities in the past nine weeks,' he said. 'My feet are reduced to ankles from trolling through *suq* after *suq*. I've loitered in *qahwas* and *maqaads* swilling coffee from *ghoum-ghoums* big enough to hide a corpse. Not a cheep about the "Prophet". Very unCairo.'

Swann gazed at him pensively. 'I said "maybe", son,' he commented.

'Meaning?'

'It would be very Cairo,' Swann said as he put on the glasses, 'if the *biqbashis* arranged a leak for you and then stepped in to claim the kudos.'

'Then why two knifers?'

'Your beauty is unimpaired, praise be to Allah.'

Silk thought about it. He shook his head. 'I see arguments against it,' he said.

'Maybe you're right. Very well. I'll send Rand here to take over from you.'

Silk stared at him. 'That nit?' he queried incredulously. 'By golly, we are scraping the bottom of the barrel.'

Swann raised his brows noncommittally. 'What about the overall situation here?' he asked gently.

'Simmering,' Silk said, worried at having to hand over to Rand. 'Any day it can blow up. This unified military command has given the *biqbashis* their chance. It's possible they'll produce enough El Qahir and El Zafir rockets to hedge Israel with launch-pads in Syria and Jordan. And the Israelis may try to forestall it.'

Later, when Swann left to catch his return plane, he asked: 'What happens if your meeting with Sabri goes sour?'

'I haven't found him yet,' Silk said. 'But I don't expect to be immortal. You'll find another sucker.'

3

THE address of Mahmoud Amer was Twentytwo, Hamadan Road. Shortly before dark Silk checked his automatic, put it back into his shoulder holster, and set off to walk there. If everything had gone according to schedule Swann should be beginning his return flight on one of those planes which gave its passengers a 'free' minikin glass of below average quality wine from nameless vineyards and a meal described as 'the fare of gourmets' which had the memorably delicate flavour and tenderness of partly manufactured indiarubber. Swann was probably playing for safety by disregarding the menu and washing his pills down with a soft fruit drink. Every migraine was misery but those which occasionally plagued Swann often assumed epic dimensions.

Silk went into the old city through Herod's Gate. To lose possible tails, he varied his pace and direction along several streets. He seemed to be less attended than the average tourist.

Every street was busy. He threaded his way past raw-voiced dealers, tatterdemalion beggars, prosperous Arab businessmen wearing Western suits, out-of-town villagers whose robes were thickly ingrained with desert dust, stocky Jordanian soldiers whose red-and-white *hatta w'aqqaal* drifted over their ears, darting shaven-headed urchins, robust housewives, priests of every Middle East origin, sightseeing Western tourists. Every Arab odour of sweat and dust, heat and leather and food, lingered along the narrow streets. At the Street of Columns he turned into the Via Dolorosa, cut across the Muslim Quarter and increased his pace. Near St. Stephen's Gate he got entangled with a party of black-hatted, black-bearded, black-habited Greek Orthodox priests. Each one of them looked like a brother of that man on Cyprus. Their voices faded as he went through the Gate.

It was dark when he headed north up Jericho Road. There were fewer people here. He met several cars and early evening buses setting off into the countryside. A convoy of military trucks full of soldiers arriving from Amman kept him on the old city side of the road. He wondered if their arrival was due to alarm or routine. After they had passed he glanced round. Nothing awoke his interest. He crossed the road and turned into one of the newer suburbs, an area of small white houses behind high walls and sprinkled with baby cypresses.

Every Middle East city witnessed the growth of similar overspill suburbs. This one resembled those outside coastal towns in the south of France. An air off the eastern deserts ended the illusion. At times its search over his face had the feverish intensity of passionate fingers eager to memorise each cherished feature. In the first road he passed two social-status cars, sleek pastel-hued beasties full of affectation of being free from inbuilt obsolescence and who looked so damn self-conscious you felt they would simper if you touched them.

This was an enclave of new-style Arab businessmen. Among them were tired men intent on building up consumer-demand for import lines. Here were ambitious minor government officials who claimed an influential cousin among the élite of Amman. You might find a new-style teacher, passionately devoted to modern education and fanatically pan-Arab. Almost certainly one house had a young Arab trained in Moscow in technical know-how.

The walk took Silk over half an hour. It gave him a chance to think over his meeting with Swann.

Hamadan Road was near the centre. The rough white walls of Twentytwo gleamed palely in starlight. They were eight feet high and divided by large wrought-iron double gates. Beyond the gates a broad drive swooped right to a garage large enough for two cars and a narrow path led to the front door. On either side of the front door were square windows. They and the uncurtained windows on the single storey above were lit by partly shaded ceiling lights.

He glanced round. Everything was still. He took another peek through the open gates. No sound reached him from the house. He took another look behind him. Some distance away a car sounded its horn.

He coughed politely and walked through the gates and up the path to the house and mounted the two shallow steps to the shiny white door with its black accessories and pressed the bell stud on the right-hand side.

Somewhere inside the house a chime of muted bells tolled mournfully. It was the only significant event. After an interval he bothered the stud again. Another carillon gave sad acknowledgment of his presence. He got older. Then he turned on his heels. The lighted windows showed patches desolate as a Japanese sand-garden and a heavy chain linking the handles of the garage doors. A paved strip more cute than crazy bordered the house.

He took the left-hand path. His careful cries brought no friendly '*Ahlan wa sahlan*—Our dwelling is as free to you as is the plain' greeting. Through the first window he saw a small study-type room where a man could shelter from female interference. Its pale grey walls enclosed a crimson divan, plump apricot-hued cushions, an Iranian carpet on which red and yellow tulips twined over a light grey ground. Down one wall hung another tulip carpet.

His calls went unanswered. As he rounded the corner of the house light coming through open french windows illuminated another cheerless strip of garden. The room was empty. Its motif was Arab. Bedu rugs abounded. Decorations on pottery grouped on low tables were copied from pre-Christian, Sumerian, Akkadian, and Assyrian designs. On one wall hung about sixty dolls wearing colourful dress, Arab, Bahai, Turkoman, Circassian, Qurd, and cuddly Greek Orthodox priests complete with beards and ornate vestments. On other tables were hand-sewn blouses, local jewellery, mother-of-pearl rosaries. Another table displayed knives and daggers. In this setting the harpsichord on the left was unexpected. It looked like a genuine Ibach.

'Hello there!' he said genially to nobody and stepped inside, turning on his heels. On one section of the wall backing onto the garden were dolls representing the Christian Mystery plus shepherds and wise men, winsome angels, a recumbent Lazarus of ghastly complexion which opened its eyes when he raised its head. He turned and went across the room. The harpsichord was an Ibach. He walked round it and ran a fingertip along sections; no dust. Another cheerful call went unanswered. He flexed his fingers. It had been a long time. He raised the lid and pulled out the stool and sat down.

An experimental canter through what he remembered of one of J. S. Bach's preludes was calculated to yank the old boy alive again to register an indignant protest so he switched to the safer realms of Scarlatti's Sonata in A Minor where finger faults often sound like the intended tinkle. Then he set about the C Minor. He got on better than he deserved. The Ibach had a lovely tone. Much encouraged, he launched into Bach's Toccata in D Major. This lively scamper had suited him while he was an outraged boy practising in obedience to the fantastic decision of his otherwise manageable parents.

At the end he sat still ignoring his audience. It had come in from the garden during the C Minor Sonata but he had paid no attention because he had never heard of anyone shooting the harpsichordist. Then he sighed and stood up, turning as he did so. Immediately he gave the start of the humble artiste hauled out of his reverie by the sight of people watching his private indulgence.

There were four of them. Three were men. They sat in

an uneven half-circle on the incongruous stiletto-leg chairs staring at him.

They were Arabs of unplaceable origin and wore anonymous dark business suits. Right of centre lolled a vast man, every ounce of twenty stone, whose heavy-lidded, protuberant eyes gave an appearance of having gazed long upon exquisite sins. His pouting lips curved disdainfully, his jowls swathed his collar like an inner tube, and a broad channel divided his hair into two vanishing islands. He was about fifty. The individual beside him obviously loathed admitting to being forty. He hoped that a moustache of the sort that Hollywood stuck beneath noses thirty years ago to indicate temperamental Latin lovers in B comedies would in his case turn an oblong face into that of a man of distinction. It needed something more, like a general overhaul and reassembly of components. At the other end of the line was a small thin man of approximately twentyfive. His narrow eyes and lips twitched and his hands fidgeted ceaselessly as if he was quarrelling with someone who never let him get in a word. His gaze flicked round the room like a bride's duster. His was the only tired and old suit.

The woman stood at the window looking out at the darkness like one of those women in Tennyson's poems. She was tallish. Her hips swelled under the slightly tight skirt with the symmetry of twin mandolines.

Silk smiled shamefacedly at the large man. 'Mr. Sabri?' he queried and went on in an abashed tone: 'I must apologise for playing your harpsichord.' He flapped his hands aimlessly. 'When no one answered the bell I came round as all the lights were on and I found the window open and this harpsichord. It was a great temptation. My father was a missionary. In Port Said.'

'You play well, sahib,' the large man said unenthusiastically.

'I haven't kept it up.'

'I am not Mr. Sabri, sahib. I am Mahmoud Amer.'

'Oh,' Silk said blankly. The huge man had an air of

authority and was the most conservative of the three; he subscribed to the ancient Arab belief that a vast belly indicated affluence and social prominence. The man of distinction was probably the most intelligent and therefore the most susceptible to fear. Both were probably regarded as cultured by their families because they used a knife for their food and urinated while standing. The smaller young man probably used his fingers for eating and squatted down to piss. Silk would not have trusted any of them. 'Oh,' he said again.

'Sabri left months ago.'

He frowned. 'How annoying,' he said. 'I was sure he lived here.'

Amer took the bait casually. 'I am not sure where he is now, sahib,' he said. His gravel-churn voice was slow but English came easily to him. He used sahib in its Arabic form of 'friend', rather than in the style of the Hindu honorific. 'Sabri is a restless man. He bought this house for his business but disliked having to remain in one place. Are you a friend of his?'

'I've never met him. I've brought him a letter from his brother.'

The last sentence laid his head neatly on the block if Amer and/or his companions mixed prophecy with dolls. Amer continued to stare at him as if he might suddenly indulge in unusual practices.

'He stayed at an hotel before he left Jerusalem,' Amer said. 'Mekki, fetch the general address-book from the office.' He might have been ordering a snail to crawl out from under a stone.

Twitching, the youngest man got up and went through the doorway which led deeper into the house.

As time went by Amer asked social questions and heard that the intruder was a reporter. Silk found his interest increasing. Mekki was taking his time. That meant he was nosing around to see if anything had been stolen or shifted round.

'I would like to have been a newspaperman,' Amer sighed.

'You haven't missed much,' Silk assured him and smiled blankly at the woman who had turned to face him.

He felt sorry for her. At around thirty she carried an intolerable burden of beauty, from classically proportioned features to the rare figure which at any given hour several hundred million women were day-scheming to achieve. She had the lot. And commonsense. She shunned eye messes, used hardly any colour on lips which had the sculptured sort of lines, wore no jewellery, let her oval fingernails go untarnished, and did her abundant black hair in an ordinary coil on her neck. Only the slight tightness of the skirt of her bronze-hued dress was wrong but the man who got fussy over what she wore really did need to consult a psychiatrist.

He kept his tongue in his mouth and let his eyes suggest that his favourite romp was with polar bears. She might be Egyptian or Lebanese. For most reasons that geography was unimportant. He had to admit that she bore a vague resemblance to Shamz. But it was superficial. Shamz was unique. This was just another woman, first-rate window-shopping. He imagined that men who had bullet-proof brains for everything else would be wet cottonwool about her.

He broke into Amer's moans about the difficulties of selling souvenirs to tourists.

'I must be inconveniencing you and Mrs. Amer. It really isn't important. I can send the letter back to Mr. Sabri's brother.'

Amer lifted a huge soft hand. 'Mekki will soon be back,' he said. 'We are pleased to welcome you here, sahib.'

The woman interposed unexpectedly. 'I am Mrs. Gohar,' she said. 'My husband and I are taking Mr. Amer out to dinner. It is his birthday.'

Her voice increased her problems. It was warm and strong. You wouldn't raise hell if it woke you a couple of hours early to hail the dawn. Her unhurried English was confident. She used the accent like wise women used perfume. The accompanying smile was a race between brevity and bleakness yet stated that when she felt an urge to operate the lingery variety something would ignite. He would lay even money that her toes were lovely too.

At hearing the name Gohar the man of distinction jerked up his head and gave Silk a pregnant stare. Then he resumed his keen contemplation of urgent private thoughts.

Silk nodded mildly at the woman and gave Amer his sunniest smile. 'Well well well, congratulations,' he said.

Amer raised his brows an inch. He shook his head fractionally. 'Mr. Gohar and his wife enjoy anniversaries,' he said lugubriously.

Once again the embellished face rose to give another significant glance.

Another five minutes drooled past in small talk. Then Amer said: 'Here is Mekki.'

Silk had heard the door open. Still twitching, Mekki went past and gave Amer the file. It was foolscap size, dark green, and too bulky to get lost from sight. As Amer laid the file on his gigantic thighs Silk got out his diary and ballpoint pen. Amer flicked pages slowly till he discovered loose papers. He shuffled through them. At length he glanced up.

'Mr. Sabri stayed at the Isis Hotel after he left here.'

Silk wrote it down. 'Where is it?' he asked.

'Halfway up Lawrence Road on the right-hand side. Near the Convent of Saint Agnes.'

'How do I get there?'

'Buses go near it. You'll find them outside the Damascus Gate.'

'If you go by car drive up Nablus Road,' Mrs. Gohar added.

Silk wrote it down and shut the diary. He put it and the ball-point away and stood up. 'You've been most helpful,' he said to Amer. 'I apologise for the intrusion. The harpsichord was a great temptation.'

They kept on sitting.

'Someone told me Sabri left Jerusalem months ago,' Amer said heavily. 'If I hear where he is can I get in touch with you?'

'How kind of you. I am at the Rosetta. My name is Silk.'

'I shall remember,' Amer said. 'Remember me if you meet tourists who want high quality souvenirs.'

Silk put a convivial gleam on his face.

'I'll be at the Rosetta most of tomorrow. If you're passing, drop in. Bring whatever business leaflets you can spare. I meet lots of tourists.'

'I will send you samples,' Amer said and let his head give one tiny bob. It ended the encounter like the slap of a store shutter finishing business for the day.

'Well,' Silk said brightly, 'thanks again. Good night.'

Amer nodded again.

As Silk went out into the garden their attentive silence hovered over him like gulls winging above an outward-bound ship.

He stepped briskly forward through darkness of sharper intensity than earlier. Memory guided him back to the open gateway. No footsteps whispered after him. He wished he could have bugged the room. Their present conversation might be of interest.

Outside the gates he stopped briefly to admire the outsize American car parked there.

It took him half an hour to reach the Isis Hotel.

4

You had to make allowances for such places. They were symptomatic.

Every country on every continent had been unprepared for the tourist explosion of recent years. As yet few Arabs were capable of thinking of the human comforts of other races. For them and others modern methods were still associated with Europeans. Many despised those who found money to build lavish hotels which catered exclusively for *el qhara ferenghi*, the vile infidel. Many who had money feared what would happen if it was invested in such hotels on the day that the *ji'haad*, the holy war, was finally launched upon those *jellah Yahudi*, camel-dung Jews, as the 'Voice of the Arab' promised day after day. Far more lacked the knowhow for running such hotels. Consequently, apart from such places as Cairo and Beirut and Tehran, most hotels were of the homely inn type which provided simple hospitality. The Isis was outside the description. It catered for the poorer Europeans searching for local colour and for Arabs with holes in the soles of their one pair of shoes.

He passed its entrance twice without seeing it. A belated flash of inspiration led him back to its unattractive doors. One of them screeched open at pressure from his shoulder. He found himself inside a small lobby which someone had recently painted an unwholesome yellowish-brown. The summer night heat had the flies dipping on tipsy wings. A beautiful Isfahan carpet of the wrong blue and greens for the rest of the décor was littered with pale skeletal furniture laid out to infuriate anyone hastening to the passageway on the right or the narrow staircase on the left. Hillocks of old magazines rose on the tables. Right of centre was an imitation leather, imitation easy chair. The plump little man who perched on its edge like an unlucky punter waiting to see his bookie was reading the Arabic edition of *China Reconstructs*. The reception office kept itself hidden.

As he glanced round one squad of flies went off upstairs and another squad came down like ice hockey teams changing over. His cautious sniff told him that a lot of the wrong sort of scent on the wrong sort of woman had passed this way but you might be incorrect about the latter guess here.

He heeled round. The small Arab had raised a chubby baby face and was studying him with wistful absorption. As their glances met the Arab squirmed on his fat bottom and his soft lips puckered. He had long passed his prime as a *dhakar bint*, dancing boy prostitute, but was full of hope. He diverted his gaze shyly. His plump fingers trembled and an indelicate moisture oozed out on his narrow forehead. Beyond him was a varnished brown door.

Silk got to the door without causing worse damage than severe emotional strain about his precise intentions. It led into a pink-walled lounge whose heavy dark furniture huddled into one corner like village widows agog over the latest scandal. On one wall hung a large healthily coloured portrait of the Egyptian President beaming at him as if they were old school chums. He shut the door and went to investigate the passageway. Halfway along it he discovered a shuttered eighteen-inch square hole in the left-hand wall. He had to bring his face down level with it. Behind it voices speaking Arabic were discussing the latest Saudi Arabian intrigues.

At his third rap the voices went silent. He rapped again. Seconds later the hatch was unlatched and creakled back. Close to his face hung the heavily moustached face of a stooping Arab of indeterminate age. Beneath the scimitar moustache spread a bright smile.

'*Salaam aleikum*,' the man said.

'*Mah aleikum*.'

'You are too late foah accommodation tonight, sah. I may be able to get you niz bedroom in respectable private haus. If you want.'

Silk said he did not require a room and shifted his position slightly. Beyond the shadowy face was an office. On the right facing left were motionless neck to thigh chunks of two men wearing brown suits. 'I'm looking for Mr. Sabri,' he said.

'Mistah Sabri came back yesterday, sah.'

'Is he in?'

'He may hev come in, sah.'

'Will you find out?'

'Sah, we have no bedroom telephones. Mistah Sabri is in roam one-oh-six. He has his roam-key.'

'Shall I go up?'

'Yes, sah.'

'How do I find it?'

'Tahn right on the fast landing, sah.'

'Thanks,' he said.

Directly he turned back up the corridor the shutter jerkled back over the hatch. At once the voices resumed their discussion. All three were excited. Jerusalem Arabs felt peculiarly involved in every event which affected the contemporary Muslim world. This trio were as talkative as budgerigars raised on Purple Heart pills.

The lobby had its one occupant, now the symbol of wounded sensitivity, doing a cooling-off lap round the furniture. He avoided its reproachful eyes on his route to the staircase.

Staircase was really a high-flown description. Two people of ordinary width who got past each other on its steps would carry away an intimate knowledge of how life had shaped the other. Each step had its short central strip of bile-tinted linoleum nailed down to protect boards which wheezed like failed sopranos. The layer of dust had been undisturbed since the original builders provided it. Illumination came from one naked bulb over the landing. At the top faded blue carpeting lay along the passage which led back to a point above the lounge where it divided in a T shape. At either end were single electric light bulbs whose manufacturers' claims were defeated by the roasted corpses of flies filming each bulb.

The boast represented by the o in one-o-six was somebody's dream. There were eight doors. On his left a short passage was ended by a beige wall on which hung a magazine portrait of the Pan-Am building with the rest of New York respectfully absent. At the end of the right-hand passage were the bottom two steps of an even narrower flight leading up between shadowy walls to the second floor. Somewhere one blustery radio voice held forth. Elsewhere another voice scratched at its owner's problems. He chose the right-hand passage, went unsuccessfully to the steps and peered up into darkness. He went back down the other branch. Room one-o-six was the second on his right. It must overlook the road.

He glanced at the ceiling while he waited. Somebody was inside the room. He heard footsteps go across carpet. He eased his shoulders and hoisted an all-purposes smile. This was unlikely to be an easy interview. He rapped on the door. Its lock was keyless.

An impressive length of silence suggested that Somebody wasn't there any longer.

He rapped again and said: 'Mr. Sabri?' As he spoke he took hold of the oldfashioned white porcelain doorhandle. It gave easily. He followed it into a small hot grey cell which had just sufficient appropriate furniture to qualify it for the description of bedroom.

The woman who lounged on the once white coverlet spread over an iron-frame single bedstead facing the door looked at him idly. Almost absentmindedly she drew her loosened dark brown silk blouse over her breasts and commenced to fasten its buttons. She had beautiful slender hands of the sort which should always do graceful things.

He kept his smile unsurprised. 'I came to see Mr. Sabri,' he said.

'He is out.'

'Have you any idea when he will return?'

'No.'

He decided that the description of woman implied too many years. She was a physically neat girl of about twenty-four who looked like the girl next door back home at the age of sixteen. Her deep voice was in piquant contrast to her lean boyish features and short-cut untidy black hair. She created a Western impression by more than the brown linen coat and skirt, smoke-toned nylon stockings and tiny dark shoes with fashionable heels. Her eyes were rather special. They had the heavy-lidded gaze which Middle Eastern women got free at birth; genteel British novelists once called such eyes slumbrous though the last thing they suggested was that their owner got much sleep. There was another significant feature; American women have an unmistakable quality, and she had it. The large brown handbag resting against her right thigh gaped wide open.

She did her best to conceal her fear. He was aware of it like an animal reaction as if the hair rose on the back of her neck at the sight. That was natural. He recognised her. While they spoke he noted she wore this attire with the same authority that she had worn local robes when they faced each other two nights ago. On balance he preferred her without the wig and those large hollow-circle earrings. She increased his conviction that she was the same girl. As they looked at each other he saw her eyes gain confidence, as if she believed that he did not recognise her. She sat on the tidy bed trying to appear at ease, two buttons of her blouse still unfastened, but with her shoes on. Curiouser and curiouser.

She sat up unwillingly. 'Is there anything I can do?' she asked without relish.

'A mutual friend asked me to see him when I got here.'

'Have you had a long journey, Mr.——?'

'Silk. I've come from Cairo. Do you think he'll be longer than half an hour, Mrs. Sabri?'

She ignored the chance to admit or deny the status given her. His very best smile set to please won him total indifference. She sat unresponsive under his admiration of her gamin charm and those beautiful hands and the gentle rise and fall of the suntanned breast under the thin blouse.

'He may come back at any time,' she said. 'I wish I knew when he will come.' She spoke slowly, each syllable given its English intonation as if she was afraid of lapsing into mission-school accents if she let herself hurry. 'You know how it is.'

He tch-tched commiseration.

'It's idiotic. Business should be restricted to business hours. This is the greatest age of slavery the world has known. Everyone chases the carrots or carats dangled in front of their noses.'

She widened her eyes. 'Are you a philosopher, Mr. Silk?' she asked politely.

'Good gracious, no!' he exclaimed and hovered over the atrocious pit of autobiography. 'Well, I'd better wait downstairs. Forgive me for disturbing you, Mrs. Sabri.'

She stood up. Although the fashionable heels gave assistance the crown of her head was barely above the level of his shoulders. The hemline of her skirt was low on her calves. 'He may be back very late,' she warned. 'I expect you are busy. Where can he contact you?'

'I'm at the Rosetta. Will you ask him to call me?'

She flicked away cats-tongues of hair fallen over her forehead. 'The Rosetta,' she said. 'I will tell him.'

'Thanks.'

'Oh,' she said casually as he turned away. 'What was the name of your mutual friend?'

He wheeled towards her, smiling and vaguely touched by how she did her best in a situation which had caught her unawares. Everybody had to begin somewhere. Just this once she would have sympathy from every experienced agent. Not much sympathy. Not the sympathy which wrenched your bowels or laid your liver on the block ready to be cut into tender bleeding slices. Just a stir of plain vocational sympathy with one pinch of amazement thrown in because she lacked the mannerisms of women agents.

'Ah yes,' he said and was interrupted. Without her thigh for support her do-it-yourself kit toppled off the bed and its contents were strewn over the floor. He saw three white handkerchieves, two of them unfolded, and a small red plastic comb, several letters, a room-key with a metal tag, four lipstick containers, an oblong bag mirror, a leather fold full of paper money, a gilt compact which spilled powder on the carpet, the starveling type of address-book where women store their personal dynamite, and one baby automatic. Coins scurried out of sight like scared mice.

Her feet went towards the automatic. He caught hold of her.

'Careful,' he said, let go of her, and went down on his knees.

The top letter came from Cairo. It was addressed to M. Nazra Abbas at the Saladin Hotel, Jerusalem, and had been franked four days ago. The automatic was of Japanese manufacture. Its safety-catch was on and the metal felt cold to his touch. He handled it carefully because you could never be too cautious about these trinkety gadgets.

As she knelt beside him he uttered hearty male noises. Temporarily her concentration was on holiday. There was no interference as he reached for the up-ended kit-carrier. Its large red silk-lined pouch contained other coins, an old mother-of-pearl pen-knife, and nail-scissors. Its other compartments were zipped shut. He stuffed the letter and automatic into it and set it on the floor between them.

'*Mahleesh*,' he kept repeating cheerfully, 'never mind. These accidents happen.'

He shunted about collecting things. For once he was so helpful that he qualified for his Wolf Cub badge. The girl followed him around muttering embarrassment. When he was sure she was not searching for something which he had failed to see he slackened his pace and half crept under the bed collecting miscellaneous coins. Then he crawled back and got up. He helped her to rise.

'You shouldn't carry an automatic in your handbag,' he chided friendlily. 'It's very dangerous. There can be a nasty accident. . . . I must go. Oh yes, our mutual friend. His name is Ali Thani.'

She did her present best to smile casually. 'I shall remember,' she assured him.

He smiled and nodded, turned on his heel and left the room.

Down in the lobby the chubby Arab sat glowering peevishly through a *Time*-style Indian newsmagazine left by someone. He raised his head to gaze significantly at Silk and at the same instant the doors leading from the street opened and a man strode in, turned to shut the doors emphatically as if afraid they might be blown off their hinges, then swung round to survey the scene. Silk sighed. The man was thirtyish, less than average height but of muscular build, his straddle stance on the mat suggesting he might do nonchalant physical jerks to keep fit. He looked very keen. His shining black hair was neatly parted, his broad face glowed. His shirt was white, his tie saffron, his suit blue, and someone had shone his shoes. He was Chinese.

Silk slouched to the pile of magazines on one table and the Chinese strode across to the Arab. The former had every outward sign of one who thought himself one of the master race. The genial smile which suddenly spread over his face was out of keeping with his military bearing.

He halted beside the quivery Arab and asked: 'Are you Mr. Sabri?'

His English was confident.

'I am Isa el Fattah,' the Arab said with fluttery sweetness. He stood up, swaying, doing his damnedest to appear fragile. 'Mr. Sabri is a guest here. He——'

'Where can I find him?'
'He is out. He——'
'Where is the reception office?'
Silk took himself off.

Outside the hotel two habited Franciscan monks paced past him engaged in an intricate theological discussion conducted mainly in French. While the faint slap of their sandalled feet died away he paused to admire the evening.

In the last half-hour the land smell of burnt saucepans had grown stronger, hanging like rows of fusty old curtains strung between cypresses lining both sides of the road. Where visible amid skeins of high thin cloud the stars had the crinkled glint of well-used cooking tin-foil. Although the Chinese had strode into the hotel importantly there was no sign of a car. He thought that unusual. According to his observations officials of what Peking called 'the newly emergent forces' usually took their cars for nice drivies on business calls.

He padded across the road. On the other side he strolled fifty yards down it and then retraced his steps and went fifty yards up it past the hotel. Nobody had left a car here but there were other roads nearby. He found a tree from where he could see the hotel entrance and leant his back on it.

Several things occupied his attention. If you are an agent killing time under a tree you always have things to think about. Chiefly people, odd people, vast men who manufactured dolls, a girl who did everything wrong, men who went away and came back and went off to unstated destinations, a Chinese who marched about like a soldier or somebody escaped from the League of Health and Beauty. Other people.

There are dangers to thinking too deeply when you stand under a tree at night.

He heard two soft footsteps behind him. But there was a communications breakdown between his ears and his brain. He went on thinking. There was another tiny footstep like the fairy must take to get on top of the Christmas tree. His mind came awake. It was too late. Pain from the blow on his head whipped down to his heels. His knees buckled. Another blow cracked down on his head.

Then everything was splintered black chips swirling round him.

5

EVERY so often the night flapped at his eyes like a black curtain which someone was shoving over his face. A jazzy big beat dinned through his head. That worried him. Evidently you grew sensitive about such treatment when middle age tiptoed leering towards you.

The man sitting beside him on the driver's seat of the car gave a theatrical sigh. He kept doing it. 'I just can't figure out why you're so goddam uncooperative,' he complained. He pronounced can't as cant and figure as fig-ewer. His speech was full of American pronunciations and turns of phrase to which he lent a rough intonation to bear witness to his own virile masculinity. 'When I offer you a private deal strictly on the level which will save both of us trouble, why the hell do you play coy?' he asked aggrievedly.

'I dislike deals which start with battery and assault.'

'Oh, for chrissakes! Must you go fancy pants on me?'

'What an awful expression. How often must I tell you I don't know what you're talking about? Your imagination is far too lurid.'

Another sigh came through the darkness.

'Okay okay, you want we start again. You are Dorian Silk.'

'Yes.'

'You're British.'

'Much to my pleasure.'

'Yeah, so you said. You were part owner of a travel agency.'

'More or less correct. It was a company which ran its own tours.'

'Now you're supposed to be a newsman.'

' "Supposed to be" is incorrect. I am. You can read my pieces if you read the right periodicals. They're very good.'

'Okay, stuffed shirt, have it your way. You are also a British agent.'

'Incorrect,' Silk said thoughtfully. 'I agree you might assume I am an agent as you call it. What an unfortunate description, isn't it? It sounds like someone who sells rubber goods or patent medicines, doesn't it? Anyway, here I am in the Middle East if you see what I mean and will forgive the misnomer. So wrong, isn't it? The old term of Near East was pretty daft—why not Near India or Nearer Asia —but Middle East is quite preposterous.' He spoke rapidly, words spilling out of his mouth while he thought of other things. 'It's nowhere near the middle. And you'll agree the East doesn't even begin here. That yarn about Istanbul being the gateway to the East is old codswallop. People who believe that in this age will believe anything.'

'Listen, Silk——'

'Shut up, Dominis,' he snapped irritably. 'I've sat here while this headache you've given me has grown worse and while you've waved that revolver at my face. I've been pretty patient listening to you babble bilge about my being a spy while my friends wait for me at the hotel.'

'You weren't busting a gut to meet them.'

'What a horrible phrase! Does it concern you or anyone if I hang round for five minutes because I want to decide if I shall date a woman? She would have been out within minutes. Instead you cosh me so you can unload this bull about my being an agent.'

'Silk——'

'My turn, Dominis. If that is your name. Where did you get such an idea? Did you or one of your friends ever see me having a drink with Kim Philby at the St. Georges in Beirut? An association of ideas? Old, mate. Several people have thought I might be one of those spy blokes. They were wrong too. I get around because I'm a newsman. But those people never bludgeoned me to try to prove their theory. You're ingenuous, mate.'

At the core of the silence which followed that lot was a suffering man. It was not himself. He was poised ready to carry on.

The sufferer had introduced himself as an American citizen by name David Dominis of Washington, D.C.

Mr Dominis was an impressive figure. When he took off his shoes and clothes he certainly topped six feet four and weighed upward of two hundred and twentyfour pounds devoid of an ounce of fat. He had a jaw like a train buffer. Nature had designed his square teeth to snap park railings as if they were cheese straws. Each of his grey eyes jutted forward in the style of oldfashioned car headlights. His skin had an olive pallor. You got an impression that under the neat dark suit and white shirt with its circumspect black and gold tie was one of those bodies which could flex every muscle at order. A near crew-cut gave his curly black hair the appearance of coiled wire.

In short, Dominis was like one of those college football huskies photographed in full colour and armour for the *Saturday Evening Post* at the onset of the pigskin season. He was several years on from that phase, one of those men whom sad chorusgirls daydream about while they charm bald patrons blessed with healthy bank balances. His strong voice was full of deep resonance. His Americanism was emphatic. He put it on parade like one of those high-strutting drum-majorettes in action along Main Street. He created an atmosphere of being what writers for women's slick-paper magazines called 'a great hunk of man', which deepened the mystery of why he should act like an emotional nit.

At present he reposed behind the wheel, body half-turned so he could see Silk, left forearm resting on the back of the seat, right arm on the wheel and the revolver in its hand clear in the dashboard lighting. He had taken Silk's gun and slid it into the right-hand pocket of his jacket.

Silk gazed through the windscreen at tinselly stars above the dark hump of the Mount of Olives and thought his thoughts. He had been brought here while half conscious, presumably for Dominis to propose his deal.

The resonant voice interrupted his thoughts.

'I'm suggesting we save ourselves time and money.'

'I heard you. Must we go over it again? I've no doubt you are, as you imply, a member of your Central Intelligence Agency. You mean that or you mean nothing. But I am not a British agent.'

'You surely are.'

'I'm not, you know. So the reason for a deal is out.'

Dominis was a trier. 'Are you afraid it's unethical?' he asked. 'Hell, other guys do it every week.'

Silk seemed to be expected to say something so he said: 'Ah.'

'Okay then. Aw c'mon, fraternisation starts at our level. If men like us on the job can't discuss mutual problems, what chance have those guys back in Washington and London? Hell, be sensible. I'm bushed and I guess you are too. Just tell me the details and we can go home.'

'The British intelligence service would have to go pretty low to get me onto its pay-roll. I work for my keep.'

Dominis veered onto a new tack. 'Most guys who get clobbered are more mad than you,' he commented.

'If I interpret that correctly . . . you would know. Whatever the cause, you've got delusions. I have to humour you. Now let me out of this car like a good boy and we'll forget the whole thing.'

For the ninth or tenth time, maybe more, Dominis said: 'You're after the Prophet.' His show of sweet reasonableness was as strong as an old nylon after the puppy had chewed it for a week. 'So am I. I've been chasing the Prophet for months.'

'He's been dead for centuries.'

'He is the biggest menace out here for years.'

'The one Prophet I know about is Mahomet.'

'Ah, for chrissakes, must you act like a prissy schoolmarm?' Dominis demanded exasperatedly. 'You know about the Prophet. You know unless he's stopped, and fast, we'll have trouble right through the Arab world. C'mon, Silk. Be realistic.'

He was getting rattled. The affability was thin on top.

'This chap you're talking about is completely new to me,' Silk said wearily. His career as an actor had been fragmentary but this situation did not call for an Olivier or a Jean-Louis Barraud. Even so, the situation was delicately balanced, the ploy against him. 'I doubt if he exists outside of your imagination.'

'Then why do you waste time following him around?'

Silk lifted a hand and then exclaimed: 'Damn it, surely I can scratch without you brandishing that thing at me?'

'You might want to scratch me.'

'Whatever gave you the idea I'm in love with you?'

'Two ha-has. Pretty sure of yourself, aren't you, Silk?'

'Surer of me than I am of you and other lunatics.'

'You've visited at least ten cities from Marraqesh to here in the last few weeks. Don't deny it. Why?'

'Surprise surprise. Newsmen get around. I must remember to take those pills for invisibility.'

Dominis glared at him through the milky light. 'One of these days,' he said heavily, 'I'll fix me a wooden figure of a Limey, old school tie, bowler hat, the lot, and fill it with holes.'

'Revolver or rifle? Tell me, how does one fill something with holes? Now, let's shake hands and go home, huh? I'm hungry.'

Dominis drew in air like a man breaking surface after a deep, deep dive. 'Okay,' he said wearily, 'we'll sweat it out here. I guess even you can't talk bull all night.'

'You underestimate me. I'm wonderfully adaptable.'

He plugged away at it for some while. Dominis bore it with a show of manly tolerance. Then his patience began to show signs of wear and tear. At first it was a slight shift of his hips, then his far knee jiggled. Later his hands flicked along his muscular thighs in a stylised gesture. Finally his self-control broke.

'Drip,' he interrupted succinctly. 'Wake up, Silk. You Britishers don't give orders now.'

'Ah.'

'The sun has set on your empire, feller. Sorry—Empah.'

'Ah?'

'You're down to those foggy pimples of rock off the coast of Europe. Plus your quaint traditions and lousy plumbing.'

'Ah, I know! You're trying to win friends and influence people!'

'I'm telling you, feller, your country will never be important again. No power, no real money. You're archaic. You've had it. The long dark night has settled over Britain. You need friends.'

'Oh, I know. You're one of those who criticise our Empire and French overseas possessions. There was the Pax Britannica, yes? Quietness in India, and Nepal, and Central Asia. Places around here. I do hope the American taxpayer is happy now that there is no Pax Britannica.'

'We won't go into that,' Dominis said primly. 'I'm telling you that nowadays your country takes orders. You'd better accept it. Since you've gotten yourself into this affair wise up and be smart.'

'You've forgotten to say "or else",' Silk said reproachfully, and heaved himself unhopefully at the other man. He saw no alternative likely to free him. Although the wheel hampered him he had one slight advantage over the other man. He didn't care what happened to the car.

Foolhardiness won its reward. The force of his fist smashing down on the other man's right forearm just above the wrist gained its immediate objective. The blow jarred the other man's tendons on the wheel and involuntarily those strong fingers jerked open. The revolver dropped onto the floor. Then his plans went awry.

As they dived for the gun an unlucky punch for him sank

deep into his stomach. Their heads crashed together. His wits went off for a drunken whirl. The gasp of pain sagged from him like a sigh. They grappled like tormented lovers. He had one of those idiotic thoughts that there were better companions for this sort of tangle. Dominis got a hold on his neck and started to use pressure on his windpipe. He held his breath, keeping control for as long as possible. Gradually his hands got past Dominis's shoulders and gripped his jaw. Dominis had sufficient knowledge of unarmed combat to realise when his jaw was near to being dislocated but his efforts to writhe free were prevented by his own plan of semi-strangulation.

Silk felt his lungs strain hurtfully. His brain seemed to be swelling. He knew he must complete his task now or have no other chance. He butted his head into the other man's face. It was the fortunate instant. He felt the fingers loosen slightly and the knee busy where he preferred to be without knees lost malice. He jabbed his head into the American's face again and was rewarded by a grunt devoid of pleasure.

At once the clinging fingers renewed their pressure. He felt the thumbs threatening to squash his Adam's apple. Redness misted his eyes. Choking, his lungs straining for air, he slid his right hand round till the heel of its palm was under the other man's chin. He started to shove it up. His left hand searched vainly over the floor. Dominis faltered, unable to decide whether he should throttle or writhe free from the weight pinning him down.

Silk felt a fingernail of his left hand scratch over steel. He let his energy go in a burst of action, working like a maniac. He scooped up the revolver, jerked his head aside and swiped the barrel of the weapon along the other man's jaw. The grasp on his neck lessened. He struck again. Dominis gave a moan. His hands fell.

Coughing and gulping air, Silk switched the revolver to his other hand and jammed it into the other man's ribs while he fumbled in the right-hand jacket pocket and got out his automatic. Instantly he heaved himself off the opposition. He breathed awkwardly, unable to get air deep into his lungs. His throat ached like an exposed nerve. The red fringe to weird black shapes falling in front of his eyes gave them an appearance of Abstract art. It was some consolation that Dominis was feeling worse. He had slumped on his side and kept groaning.

Silk massaged his neck gingerly. 'We could get paid for this sort of thing in Japan,' he whispered weakly.

He slid back across the seat. He was getting too old for cowboy and Indian games. Wearily he undid the door and half fell into the Middle East version of fresh summer night air. For a moment he stood unsurely, gulping air down his aching throat, a gun in each hand. Then he shut the door and went round the back to get into the driving seat. As he reached the rear the engine came alive. The car started immediately.

He could have run. He could have shot at the tyres. Instead he stood still watching it go. There was cause to assume he would meet Dominis again. The man had left several matters wide open.

He gazed vacantly at the disappearing rear light. Then he was running fell pelt across the road trying to escape from the headlights which had come on from behind and pinned him like a butterfly in their glare. The car howled at him like a shell. He only just got to the nearest tree and sprawled full-length beyond it. The car hurtled on down the road.

When he struggled up onto his knees both of them had vanished in the darkness.

6

HE STOOD back among shadows of the tree waiting to get his wind. His throat ached vilely. His head felt as if somebody had tested it for a major demolition job.

He heeled round peering at adjacent darknesses. If anyone else nearby disliked him they were keeping their presence secret. There was quietness beyond the tom-tom pound of blood in his ears. It left him unsatisfied. He slid the revolver into the left-hand pocket of his jacket and thumbed off the safety-catch of his automatic. Carefully, poised for possible reactions, he reached out his right foot and scraped it on the ground. It fidgeted over a ridge of grit mixed with broken stones thrown up by passing traffic. If anyone near had malice intent they kept it bottled up. His two coughs died away unheeded. Minutes passed emptily.

Nonetheless as he set off to walk back he went through normal routines to disconcert pursuers.

Far off a car purred throatily along the highway to Amman. Its sound faded. The lengthening silence gave him an opportunity to get at his thoughts. Since he left his hotel they had multiplied rapidly. One style and another it had been an eventful evening. Few of his thoughts pleased him. He liked missions where he began with some knowledge of what was afoot. He disliked mysteries and cities with their inevitable rat-races of one variety or another.

Something rustled off on his left. He went swiftly into the nearest patch of darker shadow and halted. It could have been any innocent thing but he was not taking unnecessary risks.

When he went on again his mind picked over what he had learned since Swann left him. It was precious little. Others were interested in the Prophet and Sabri.

He spat disgustedly. To his chagrin he had gone into this thing. Worse, oh far far worse, he had got into it while its early symptoms were so indeterminate that they might finally prove to be any one of a dozen of the large or small power-politics intrigues forever going on in this region. It was another fair sample of what an agent came up against nowadays while on his ordinary assignments. Qualification: if he was an ordinary British agent of these years at work on at least a dozen other affairs or rumours. That was because successive British governments were miserly about intelligence work which they seldom understood unless it was dished out as light adventure novelettes for sprightly old schoolboys. None of them ever thought of the agent who had to walk home with a cracking head.

At such hours he really did see the error of his ways. In this day and age only multimillionaires and belted land-owners could afford to be patriotic. Why he and others went on doing the job on the slight off-chance of their ordinary fellow-countrymen sustaining a miracle which would enable them to put first things first, only the lunatics would know. But his countrymen were unconcerned and genuflected only to their holy status symbols, the trinity of washing-machine, car, and telly, on hire purchase for ever amen. On several points Dominis was right.

You're talking to yourself again, complained his personal gremlin.

I'm walking home alone.

You shouldn't waste energy on imponderables. Something is going on here. You have real problems. What about Mrs. Sabri, Amer, Dominis, even Mekki? How about the Chinese? That one shook you rigid for three seconds, didn't he? Oh yes, he did, because, according to Peking, mainland China can produce every drop of oil it requires from inside its own frontiers . . . why should one Chinese who had military officer stamped on him from head to foot want to see Sabri? Propaganda apart, what interest has China anywhere here except oil and to undermine Russian and American influence? Were Sabri and the Chinese just good friends? Did Amer know Sabri had returned? Wasn't it clever of Sabri to have a wife who did not look like one? And, boy oh boy, how about Mrs. Gohar? She got curious too, didn't she, you old dog? Who said they didn't believe in lust at first sight? Eh?

Half a mile nearer his bed other questions increased his irritation. To date there had been three attempts here to liquidate him. Or had there? They had been spectacularly unsuccessful. Why? If the KGB or Nassah's boys wanted to kill they had organisations capable of doing the job competently. So why warn him? On the other hand, it seemed unlikely that friends of the Prophet would give him frequent notice of their watchfulness. On another count, it was beyond reasonable doubt that this business threatened to undermine his effectiveness for his real assignment.

He chewed on that for awhile. Then he shook his head and winced. This business could make him conspicuous. But to complete his real assignment properly he must be inconspicuous. He hoped Julian Rand would get here soon. Unfortunately, Rand lacked several qualifications for this sort of job. Rand was an unlikely field agent. At birth the fates had lumbered him with a whole sideboard of gold cutlery in his mouth. He was one of those pleasant innocuous men who were usually hidden by their father's shadows till they were middle-aged and then went on until they fell into the family vault without anyone knowing about it. He foresaw plenty of trouble briefing Rand for this job. Still, there never had been or would be an agent who was perfect in every respect. Except himself, of course.

Hardly anyone passed him. After some while he put his automatic into his jacket pocket. His throat throbbed viciously.

When he got to his hotel the front doors were locked. He

waited for over ten minutes for the night-porter to respond to his rings. The man wiped fingers along his scrubby grey moustache and shook his head: at this hour it was impossible to provide food or drink. They parted sourly, the porter hurrying back to his delights while he climbed tiredly upstairs.

He unlocked the door and went in and switched on the light and locked himself in. For a moment he stood looking round. Nothing had been shifted even fractionally from how he left it. He felt almost fond of the room's simplicity and glad that he had rejected Swann's offer of accommodation at one of the more pricey hotels. This suited him. The man next door was praying. The plumbing still bubbled.

He sat down on the bed and took off his shoes and socks. His throat was still painful. He fingered it experimentally. At least he knew now, all of a sudden, that several other people took the Prophet very seriously.

After a bit he stood up and went in search of aspirin.

7

HE WAS always surprised that since the early nineteenth-century poet William Blake dashed off lines which gave an opportunity which was soon taken up there had been hardly any attempts by the pashas of Tin-Pan Alley to exploit a number about Jerusalem which could claw its way up through the charts into the soon forgotten Top Ten.

Of course, the pashas have done well from the odd spiritual disc slipped out by rich communist solo entertainers and the occasional press of choirs who have had a stab at rendering the musical injunction to citizens of Jerusalem to lift their gates and sing. That is all. However, to judge from the conduct of various Christian priests the day may soon arrive when radio disc jockeys will babble 'And now for Mrs. Betsy Floggitt who'll be a hundred and nine next Tuesday and has just come out of Newtown County Hospital—congratulations on bringing yourself back alive from those doctor-men, Mrs. Floggitt, and a big hello there to all nurses—and for all you grand grandmums here is the fab new sensation about Jerusalem sung by that blonde bomb-burst, today's outstanding vocal personality, thirteen-year-old little Eva Cain, dig that gal, disc doodlers! with the wiz backing by the Reverend Cyril Bentwhistle and his Swinging Surplices . . .' It is possible. When you see what has happened to other things, it is possible. It's apples to doughnuts that Jews and Arabs will cash in by selling such a record to Christians but they won't market one for people of their own faiths.

He was certain that a pop-number about Jerusalem would feature the morning in its lyric.

Early morning is the best hour to see Jerusalem.

Then even in midsummer a magical freshness lies upon its atmosphere of inevitability. Even its antiquity seems new.

The freshness touches everything. There is a sort of architectural poetry about this city built on its own ruins from the lovely turquoise and recently restored Dome of the Rock mosque with its soaring dome to the spire of St. John's Church which rises like a manarat and the Hebrew University. On every side pinkish-yellow stone buildings shine above cypresses and the hills look meek. You detect freshness at every corner, from Mandelbaum Gate or the Tower of Storks on the north side, beside Hezekiah's Pool and Herod's Palace close to Jaffa Gate, and on the south side near the Tomb of David on Mount Zion in Israel or across No Man's Land on the Field of Blood in Jordan. It lends magic to the battlemented city walls whose stones resemble faded chessboards. At this hour you realise that inside the old city gates and spread around them are all the ordinary human characteristics. There may be a higher degree of sanctity than is usual for cities. There are certainly higher percentages of intended sanctity and pseudo-sanctity, pseudo-sin, intolerance and bigotry. Prejudice spreads like rampant weeds. Yet while this gentlest sunshine sparkles and the oldest narrow streets are comparatively fresh, while the breeze off nearby hills and distant deserts remains mild, there is also hope. You are tempted to ignore the omens of sandbagged parapets, miles of barbed wire entanglements, gun emplacements, herds of armoured cars here on the Arab side and over on the Israeli side.

Even an intelligence agent thinks about these things. They are unusually poignant here. You wonder about how you came onto this mortal coil, why are you on it, and in what condition you will be when the bugle tootles for you. Practically everyone here is convinced that Someone will then tap them on the shoulder and give them, first, a detailed explanation of everything, and, secondly, the necessary certificates to ensure them a rewarding sojourn Somewhere Else. If you keep an humble and open mind, it seems unlikely. Still, it may be so.

He left his hotel directly he finished what its chef called an English Breakfast, hurried straightaway into the old city via Herod's Gate and set about shaking off any shadows on his heels. He felt sluggish, uninclined for physical effort. His headache was worse from a restless night. His voice was down to a whisper. His simple trust in the goodness of every man was non-existent. The early clamour confused him.

It was like wandering onto the set of yet another Biblical epic film. There were hardly any foreign tourists or Christian priests about. Out of sight the tourists yawned themselves awake while they shaved or put on their faces and the priests were at their devotions. More than at other hours, this was Arab Jerusalem.

He shoved past merchants hastening to conclude their first transactions before heat thickened along these winding streets. The men wearing shabby and often unmatched Western suits were city-dwellers, men of every shape and size, alike in restless eyes and volatile temperament. His attention was caught by vastly different men from out of town, the *fallah*, cultivators, ridden here from tiny hill villages or tribal hamlets grown around desert *wadis* to sell fruits and grain, sheep and goats. They were leathery men, lean of build, their swarthy complexions testimony of harsh sunlight and fitful winds, living the tribal life familiar to their ancestors since the Arab conquest thirteen hundred years ago caused extensive soil erosion and widespread depopulation. Others, most of them bearded, were Bedu, the eternal Arab nomads. Dust paled their cloaks. Both groups strode about their affairs like men from an earlier millenium, independent and proud as emperors. Almost every man wore a grubby red or spidery black-patterned *qeffiyah* held on his head by black *agal* circlets. There were self-styled *Sayids*, reputed descendants of Mahomet, men of importance to the people of their isolated distant villages. Among them were a few old men who had a *laffe*, white cloth, wound around their dark tarbush, identification as a man of God. One fingered a *masbaha*, the Muslim rosary, of black coral, evidence of having undertaken the pilgrimage to Mecca.

Near the markets he met larger numbers of comely dark-eyed women. Many of them were accompanied by dawdling or prancing children. One glance could separate the shy-eyed *bint* on the threshold of maturity from the *jara* whose head was full of household and family problems. Most of them left their faces uncovered but wore waist-length white head-cloths which could be draped over their faces like *burqas* to conceal them from lecherous male eyes. Widows and old bent women full of years were shapeless in rusty black *abas*. They brushed past him and mullahs fingering their beards. Each visible female face showed its inbred heritage, the calm of submission to the Word of God given through men.

He had an odd sensation of having strayed back a couple of thousand years. Tourists put it down to climate but psychiatrists, who could always dream up high-falutin labels, called it cross-cultural shock. For once he nearly agreed with the psychiatrists. What gave it a fantastic twist was one's inner knowledge that just across No Man's Land young Jewish women wore bright cotton frocks which left their arms and legs bare and their parents attended synagogues in the religious quarter of Mea Shearim, where men wore *yarmulkles*, skull caps, and some sectarians still had long Hasidic *peyos*, curls, falling in front of their ears, while at seaside towns thirty-odd miles away other young Jewish women hoarded suntans where their bikinis did not reach. Many nearby Jews were *sabras*, native-born Israelis. It was a mad world.

He turned right onto the Via Dolorosa. Outside the Church of the Flagellation, at the intersection of the Second Station of the Cross, he paused to glance round as if unsure of his bearings. Everybody was too busy to bother about him. He got out his pocket guide-book and heeled around. Two young nuns went by murmuring in Italian.

As he stood there another group of Arabs went past giving respectful salutation to white-bearded mullahs pacing through the sunlight towards St. Stephen's Gate. There was dust on the mullahs' robes but the white turbans wound around their crimson tarbushes were immaculate.

He went on past the Ecce Homo Arch, turned right past the Austrian Hospice, went up El Wad Street to the Street of Columns, and stopped to refer to his guide-book again.

He shook his head at his thoughts. The trouble throughout this region was that the Jews nearby, after centuries of persecution elsewhere, had a passionate desire to rebuild their historic homeland, and these Arabs, with equal passion and fervour, were innately suspicious of all others. That left out religion. It left out oil. It left out Russia with her history of anti-semitic activity. It left out all the tinder which could be set afire so easily. But Jerusalem did prove that few men really bore goodwill towards others except on their own terms.

There was a sudden rush of people towards him from the Damascus Gate. They had the smell of the hills and of the Jordan Valley, of dust, of leather, of oil fumes from buses which had brought them here. Among them strode a huge young African monk whose dusty robes flapped around the purple-black of his naked feet. As usual the rush divided at this point. The Arabs went off into the Muslim Quarter, the Christians down the Street of Columns to their shrines. He was ignored. Few of those around even glanced at him.

He went on, turning aside as if to return to the Muslim Quarter. Then for twenty minutes or so he kept changing his direction, doubling back on his tracks, until he finally emerged through the Damascus Gate and shoved through crowds of people and donkeys and smelly lorries and cars and watchful-eyed soldiers to the central bus terminus on Jericho Road. If anyone felt an impulse for similar athletic hurry they overcame it. He was the last one to tumble into the single-decker bus full of Arabs agog with excitement over two flaxen-haired young European girls in towelling shirts and once blue canvas shorts and rucksacks who huddled over their sunburned maps.

Half an hour later he reached the Isis Hotel again.

Morning sunshine failed to enhance its outer appearance or lend charm to its interior décor. Baby-Face had gone for a nice lie down. The flies were triumphant. He went up the dingy passage to the square hole in the wall. It was open. The face of the night rose into view like a porpoise coming up to peer round for chums. They beamed hard at each other.

'Good mawning, sah,' the receptionist said. 'By Abbas, a niz mawning, sah.'

'Marvellous,' he whispered. 'Is Mr. Sabri here?'

The receptionist donned an expression of acute sadness. 'Mistah Sabri has left, sah,' he whispered back.

'When will he be back?'

'Sah, he has left Jerusalem.'

Argument was useless.

'Did he leave a forwarding address?'

'No, sah. He left quickly.'

'Did he go by car?'

'I was not heah when Mistah Sabri left. It was befoah six o'clock, sah.'

'What will happen if I write to him here?'

They were whispering at each other like conspirators.

'He will get yoah lettah when he raytahns.'

'How often does he come?'

'Evahry eight or nine months.'

Silk nodded and got out his handkerchief and dabbed perspiration off his forehead. His head was creaking miserably. He wondered if Sabri could be classified as the late Mr., either vanished forever or destined to be found floating on the Dead Sea or pulped under fallen rocks. Bodies did stray here. He put away the handkerchief.

'Did Mrs. Sabri leave with him?' he asked.

The clerk stared at him indignantly. 'Mrs. Sabri, sah?' he queried.

'Did she accompany him?'

'This is not a hotel for wives,' the receptionist said aggrievedly. 'We nevah ahlow them into ah establishment, sah.'

As Silk turned away the receptionist called him back. 'I can ahrange foah yoh to have Mistah Sabri's room if yoh requiah accommodation, sah,' he suggested in a mild tone, studying his nails.

'I'll let you know,' Silk said and walked down the passage and out into the fresher air.

Already the heat had begun to rise. He rode back in a bus at the point of combustion from oil fumes and full of Arab women talking shrilly above the clamour of shaven-headed small boys and barefooted little girls. They curved past clusters of ruins and patchworks of recently built houses set behind uneven walls, past an olive grove, past cypresses like vigilant widows united by common tragedy, past another strip where men wearing dusty *qeffiyahs* and singlets and stained trousers clambered over scaffolding, past an old mosque and bunches of pannier-laden donkeys, past buildings which became more numerous as the bus turned into Nablus Road and reached the American Colony and turned down Saladin Road.

By the time he reached his hotel he had decided on what he should do. Nothing. From now on it was his duty to stay under cover till he could hand the whole thing over to Rand. Nothing must jeopardise his work on his real assignment. He locked himself into his room and settled down for a quiet day.

By noon his voice had returned though it squeaked alarmingly on occasion. He ate in a restaurant near to the hotel.

As he lay on his bed late in the afternoon, stripped to his trousers while he caught up on his reading, there was a tap on the door. In response to his reply the door opened and Mrs. Gohar came in. She gave an appearance of sliding through the doorway. The lock clicked softly shut as she faced him smiling uncertainly.

Even at ten feet in shadowy light he could see the bruises high on her left cheek and on the side of her forehead.

8

HE SWUNG his legs off the bed and stood up feeling a bit nonplussed. There were few countries where any woman would call uninvited on an unknown lone man. Throughout Islam the idea seemed ridiculous. Yet here she was smiling uncertainly at him.

She took two hesitant steps forward.

'*Salaamu aleikum*,' he said, 'peace upon you.'

'*Aleikumu ass alaam*,' she responded formally, 'on you peace.' Her tone was edgy. 'I was passing so I came to find out if you met your friend,' she went on in English.

'Oh, I thought I said I haven't met Mr Sabri and that his brother asked me to contact him.'

'You are right,' she said absently as she glanced round. 'I had forgotten.'

She wore a black crêpe-de-chine blouse with her lightweight black coat and skirt. One button large as a roulette-wheel held the coat at her waist. The coat fitted too snugly to conceal a gun though she might have a knife hidden most places. Her left hand held a small black handbag and a nonsense of net and ribbon edged with red which might amount to a hat. He was aware of perfume. She conveyed the air of slightly breathless tension which one associated with a woman arriving late for a rendezvous with a lover of whom she is unsure.

Her gaze went slowly over him. If she expected him to become coy and rush for a dressing-gown she was out of luck. He intended to keep the afternoon heat at bay.

'Your room is beautifully cool,' she said weakly.

'The sun goes off it quite early,' he said. Perhaps his blood-heat was intended to soar at the sight of her here or at the chance of what her expressive dark eyes might be enticed to show. He could see her other undeniable attractions. But if she had been sent here to wheedle information from him they were on the wrong wavelength. The routine was old hat, a giggle. What intrigued him were those bruises.

'Come in,' he said as if suddenly mindful of good manners. 'You took me by surprise. I didn't expect to have the pleasure of seeing you again.'

After a slight hesitation she said: 'You told us you were here.' Her voice was even weaker.

'So I did,' he agreed. He drew the coverlet straight. 'Sit down. You'll find the bed best. I can't recommend the chair. Is your husband here?'

She sat down on the foot of the bed with a sigh and laid hat and bag beside her.

'He's gone to Amman.'

'What a pity.'

'Mr. Amer took him and the others off early this morning.'

He pulled the chair over near the window and stood there. 'They must be busy at present,' he commented.

'They are often away.'

'You must enjoy travelling about.'

She smiled acidly. 'Our men haven't your indulgent attitude to women,' she said. 'My husband never takes me on his business trips. Mr. Amer wouldn't permit it.'

'Surely their business would benefit from your opinion?'

'It has never occurred to them.'

He decided to lay his head on the block and see what happened. 'As you have now been doubly kind by coming to cheer up my afternoon, how about some tea?' he suggested.

'I would like it,' she said in the same weak voice.

'Right, I'll nip down to tell them,' he said cheerfully. 'They'd be sending it up soon anyway.' While he spoke he put on his shirt, pushed the tails into his trousers, and picked up his jacket. He shrugged into it. 'Oh, if you want to get rid of the dust you'll find the bathroom is the fourth door along the corridor,' he said and left the room.

The corridor was empty. So was the landing. As he ran downstairs the lobby was deserted. He went quickly outside onto the palm-shaded short drive which led to the road. It was unoccupied. A glance from the gateway showed him only the average number of parked cars. They appeared to be deserted. On his walk back to the front doors he took his automatic from the nylon holster folded into the left-hand pocket of his jacket and put it into the right-hand pocket. At the desk he asked for tea for two to be sent up to his room rightaway. The receptionist gave him a candidly hostile stare. He forewent a chance to provide explanations.

When he went into his room she was sitting at the dressingtable, her back to him, doing her hair into a thick upright roll which left her neck bare. Her coat sprawled front down on the bed. Light from the window slid over her shapely naked arms. Within these past few minutes an unmistakeable aura of woman had come into the room, a smell of perfume heightened by physical warmth. She prompted extravagant descriptions, possessing a richness of various forms of female beauty. He shut the door and leant his back on it, watching her adroit fingers probe at her hair. Light falling on part of her face showed up those bruises.

'Did you find them?' she asked cynically.

'They may be hiding up a tree.'

'Shall I wait while you climb to find out?'

'Women like you seldom visit tramp strangers. I'm curious.'

Her fingers thrust hairs into position. Her long eyes rose to focus on his reflection in the mirror and then sank under their heavy lids. She was surer of herself now. Her casual movements were just one proof. Another was how she sat.

She was a resolutely sensual woman, conveying her humours candidly. He would be safer in armour.

'Why should they send me here?' she asked.

'They might want proof I told the truth last night.'

She lowered her arms, wiped her fingertips on a two-inch scrap of handkerchief and stood up, bending forward to study her reflection. He was given another chance to think of mandolins. Then she turned to face him. 'My reasons for coming were completely primitive,' she said candidly. 'Where did you get those bullet scars on your chest?'

'I reported the war in North Africa,' he said and took his back off the door, leaving it unlocked, and slipped the key into his trouser pocket. If anyone barged in, they could leave their fingerprints everywhere. 'It got rough.'

'Tell me about it,' she ordered. 'I like men who are men.'

Within minutes one of the porters brought them glasses of mint tea. She refused to eat anything. While they drank she said: 'Most people make the harpsichord sound like a strange piano. You make it sound like a separate instrument. Where did you learn to play so beautifully?'

He fluttered his lashes at her. 'I thought I told you,' he said. 'My father was a missionary. At Port Said. We inherited an old harpsichord which went with my father's mission. Every day I tinkled away. On my eighth birthday they almost decided to launch me as an infant prodigy. May I confirm what you've heard often already? You're extremely beautiful.'

'You're beautiful too,' she said and laughed. 'I like men who tell lies amusingly.'

'It's true. You are.'

'Accidents happen. I meant about how you play.'

He kept their conversation casual to leave himself free to think. At the back of his mind was a shrewd idea that Swann would have the frothing vapours if he chanced upon this tête-à-tête.

Outwardly her questions were innocuous. They wandered over his public life without digging for confidences.

She created an atmosphere of being at ease though occasionally her smile had an edge. Her brilliant eyes searched over him as if he was a collector's item. Sometimes her hands fluttered restlessly; you didn't think of them washing up or cooking while you watched them. Basically her attitude was that of any woman who admitted to a man that he awoke her interest. He had little difficulty in lying his way past the few questions which might turn aside into more personal conversation. She referred twice to the Israelis. He stopped that line.

'Newspapermen aren't involved, thank God,' he said, 'but if you want my opinion then I'm bewildered that so many men on both sides diminish their best efforts and ignore humanity. Ultimately they must recognise each other's humanity. Everyone here faces the same problems. Why not seek the solution together? End of lesson.'

Her smile caressed him. 'I won't blame you for the Balfour Declaration,' she promised.

'Oh good! So many do. Tell me about yourself.'

Her given name was Nofret. Memory told him it was an Egyptian name from Pharaohnic days which meant 'beautiful'. Her father had been an agent of Middle East companies in England, she told him. She said that she was born in London and educated at British schools, telling him how she was evacuated from London during the blitz. Her family returned home when she was twenty. She had been married for six years. Her voice was toneless as she gave the final item of information without additional details.

'Home,' he said. 'Egypt?'

'Yes.'

'Mmmm.'

She divined his thought unhesitatingly. 'You're thinking about what Britons call "the Suez affair",' she said.

'Mmmm.'

She raised her hands. '*Mahleesh*,' she said philosophically, 'never mind. Politicians always underestimate other countries. The world thought you lacked the courage to face Nazi Germany alone. Your government should have realized that other peoples can fight.' Her voice was even. 'But my people have been known for *buqra*.'

He wondered where this chat was leading them. *Buqra* was Arabic for 'tomorrow' and had the same psychological significance as the Spanish *mañana*. Apart from sporadic outbreaks of violence engineered by hotheads who preyed on the volatile temperament and poverty and gigantic boredom of the poverty-level fellahin, the Egyptians had combined *buqra* and fatalism for centuries. Even so, few Egyptians were philosophical about Suez.

She watched his face. '*Mahleesh*,' she repeated. 'Egypt and Britain will be friends again.'

'*Buqra fee mish-mish?*'

The phrase 'tomorrow when the apricots fruit' means a long time off if ever.

'It depends on Britain's attitude to Israel,' she said and led the conversation back to personal matters. It went on for some while but produced nothing significant.

Abruptly she stood up. 'I must go,' she almost snarled. 'Thank you for being kind. You'd better padlock your door. Englishmen always let women feel they can provide worthwhile conversation. It's flattering. And dangerous.'

He got slowly to his feet. She looked quite magnificent standing there full of defiance and anger with a touch of fury and loads of latent passion. Memory jarred him. She was about the same height as Shamz and one night during their scramble out of Afghanistan Shamz had done her hair similarly. He could almost feel the ache down his arm from the wound and driving that infernal bus. Coldness clawed inside him. It usually did whenever he thought about Shamz. Well, every man had his half dozen weaknesses. He hauled his attention back to present gorgeous reality.

She averted her eyes.

'I'm glad you came,' he said. 'You probably know newspapermen are inquisitive. What caused those bruises?'

'You did.'

'Sorry.'

'It often happens.'

He went over to her. 'Why now?' he asked.

'I spoke to you.'

'Wrong?'

'Always,' she said resignedly. 'Besides, he is very susceptible to propaganda. He is the only one of five brothers who can read but he seldoms reads anything except propaganda sent to him by men in Egypt. Until two years ago he got it from Iraq. Now it comes from Egypt.'

'Mmmm.'

'Oh, I never read it,' she said, interpreting his expression correctly. 'He spends his life hating what other men tell him to hate. So he doesn't approve of my speaking to other men, least of all Englishmen and Americans.'

'That's queer,' he said in a reasonable tone. 'I would have thought Amer would see the advantage of having you be pleasant to potential customers.'

She nodded. 'Amer likes anyone who has money,' she said. 'Money is one of his obsessions.'

'Has he others?'

'One. The usual for his sort of man.'

'Maybe one day I shall find out what sort of man he is,' he said. 'He promised to let me have samples. So I may see him again.'

'There is little to find out,' she said disdainfully. 'His family has always been in trade. His ancestors worked the caravan routes. He can relate incidents which happened to his great-grandfather or his great-great-great uncle. He has their liking for boys.'

'Is that why you dislike him?' he asked amusedly. 'It's pretty common out here.'

She shook her head. 'Until three years ago Gohar had courage,' she said bitterly. 'He is intelligent. He was kind. Then Amer got hold of him. Amer is cruel and *jabbah*, tyrannical. He likes to feel supreme among his dolls, his painted boys, everyone. He turns men who work for him into creatures without character. They become afraid of losing their job and having him blacken their names. He is wealthy and a good businessman. He is always thinking of new schemes. But Gohar should have left him long ago.'

He expressed sympathy. 'Is it a family business?' he asked.

She shook her head. 'Amer's brothers have other businesses,' she replied.

'Oh, he has brothers.'

'Eight full brothers.'

'Ah-ha. And another business for a rainy day, uh?'

'They say he owns a whorehouse in Amman.'

'Mmmm,' he commented. 'Is it really possible to think up new schemes for raising money by selling dolls? I suppose there must be but I can't see it. I just haven't got that sort of mind.'

She smiled at him. 'Your work gives you another sort of reward,' she said and for an instant he thought he had given her the wrong prompt. Then she went on: 'The warehouse is full of dolls he buys from India, Burma, China, Iran, Ceylon, all over Asia.'

'Good gracious.'

An edge of cynicism tinged her smile. 'Wealthy European and American travellers buy them and pretend they've been to those countries,' she told him. 'He has other novelties too. His own house is full of them. He lives in Amman. He bought the house in Hamadan Road and we'll live there until he gets tired of Gohar.'

'Tell me,' he said thoughtfully, 'which sort of samples should I get from him? There must be some special ones.'

'The Christian dolls are very popular. So are those from Iran and the Chinese ones in regional dresses from Yunnan and Shensi and Szechwan. I prefer those he imports from Ceylon. They are beautiful. Their dresses are exquisite.'

He nodded. 'I'll remember,' he said. 'Well, I'm sure something better will turn up for you. You can get him away from Amer.'

She shook her head. 'Nothing can improve it,' she said flatly.

'You'll see,' he said confidently and his right hand cupped her chin and tilted her face up. She breathed sharply. Her heavy lids came down over her unsteady eyes. She let him turn her head to see the bruises clearly. Several were worse than he realised at first, partly hidden by skilful use of cosmetics. Two under fine hair on the side of her forehead were connected by thin cuts due to rings. There was another on her neck.

When he took his hand away she remained motionless close beside him. Her lids glistened dully. He smelt her perfume. And the physical warmth of her. Perhaps he was not as old as he felt sometimes. He thought resolutely of Swann and other saintly figures. She opened her eyes and gave him a rueful smile.

'I bruise easily,' she said.

'Tell me, why did you come here?'

Her eyes searched his. 'You attract me,' she said candidly. 'I might as well have the satisfaction of having caused it. Tomorrow or next week, soon, something I say or do will cause it again.' She hesitated. 'It isn't his fault. People pour propaganda into him. Amer robs him of independence. And he believes I've failed him.'

'Have you?'

She smiled vaguely. 'Gohar wanted fine, brave, strong, intelligent sons to inherit his wonderful propaganda future,' she said. 'He still does. They will never come. He is *ahjir*, impotent. Pride tells him I must be responsible. At first I told him to take other wives. It enraged him. He has *dam ta'eel*, heavy blood, you understand? He nearly killed me.' She shrugged. 'He cannot resign himself to his limitations.'

'Sorry,' he said again.

She drew a quick breath. '*Ahruth*,' she said curtly, 'I go.'

He did some double-thinking. 'Drop in again if you have an opportunity,' he invited.

'How long will you be here?'

'Probably a couple of days.'

'When will you return?'

He speeded up his thinking. 'Well, you know how it is for tramp reporters,' he said. 'Here today, there tomorrow. Pretty soon on the moon. Next stop, the farthest corner of the universe to await the arrival of the supreme flower of creation, Man. . . . I expect I'll be back in about six months, maybe seven.'

She flinched. 'So long?' she muttered and fell towards him. Swann would have taken three brisk steps backward rather than interfere with the law of gravity but he caught hold of her, felt her impatient fingers undo his shirt buttons to shove aside the thin material and the warmth of her naked arms twining round him to spread her hands down his back. She held herself away while her urgently whispering voice entreated his hands on her. Though he knew she wore precious little under what was visible he had a sensory shock at finding it was damn nearly non-existent. Her head went back on her neck. As she shut her eyes a taut smile flickered over her face. Her lips parted directly his touched them. It was like setting off a fire-bomb.

He kept his arms round her. He found it harder to keep a hold on himself. It had been over a year since he held a woman. He felt the doorkey burn in his pocket. She clung to him as if he was a cherished dream, her mouth wide and tender and wet. Then her mouth left his for her lips to go over his neck, murmuring endearments in Arabic, a language which had poetic extravagances and much candour for communicating the intimacies of lovers. She had every fine incitement of recklessness to ensure complaints were unnecessary.

When she raised her head a smile curved her moist lips. Her eyes moved behind their closed lids. 'O man, what a lover thou must be,' she whispered huskily, 'thy arms are like steel and the touch of thy hands like velvet. I can tell the hardness of thy loins. The wine of thy mouth makes me drunk with desire for thee.'

In the same language he said: 'Thou, woman, would be a memorable lover for every man for thy passion lights unquenchable fires to possess thy unforgettable beauty.'

She moaned pleasure. 'I need to drink beneath thy shadow,' she murmured, and her hand drew his head down to her clinging obsessive mouth. He was aware of his goodhumour going on holiday.

That saved him. Somehow he kept his sanity and despite her broken murmurous resentment managed to free his head. She hung onto him, her body a weakness devoid of strength, her face fallen on his shoulder while she struggled for breath. Without question she welcomed the consoling stir of his hands. Nervelessly she twisted for him to gather memories.

Neither of them spoke for some while but at length she raised her head and whispered: 'Why?' Her voice was dry as old paper.

He retreated into English: 'The nightclub song that an Englishman needs time is very appropriate.'

She nearly smiled. He kept hold of her, heedful of the need to keep her content through this return to reality. She enjoyed his caresses. So did he. Sort of.

Finally she drew away. 'I will try to come here again, *insh' Allah*,' she said huskily and kissed him again. Her mouth gave every promise. Then, in a harsher voice, she said: '*Ahruth.*'

'Go in peace.'

'*Allah yahafadhak*—remain in the safe keeping of God.'

She collected her things together, stood at the dressing-table for some moments to prepare for her journey back, and then gave him a steady significant glance. A moment later her footsteps hastened off down the corridor.

He wiped his forehead. It had been a damn near thing. He viewed their next meeting with concern.

He heeled round slowly sniffing at the air. It had the smell of her scent and living warmth. They were in his nostrils, on his chest. He sniffed at his hands. There too.

He grunted. Abruptly he set about stacking tea-things on the tray, put his typewriter into the wardrobe, got out his shabby suitcase and took out his old pack of cards. He cleared a space on the bed. Sitting cross-legged on it, he shuffled the cards and dealt out a hand of clock patience.

Some while later he remembered that the last time one of his hands of clock patience came out was even longer ago than the last time he touched a woman. To be precise, nearly seven years. Then he had not even met Shamz.

He raised his head to sniff the air. The presence of this woman was still on the air around him. He dealt out another hand of patience. It gave him a chance to think of other things.

9

AFTER a while he tossed aside his unhelpful pack of cards. He got up and prowled around frowning at the floor. This warm air damn nearly enshrined its recent injection of unadulterated femaleness. Nothing helped him. He was too damn human.

He rubbed his forehead. This was an hour when he needed extra wits. Snobmass, the ooooooh school of popular opinion which believed anything provided it was yapped by fashionable voices, subscribed to the notion that every intelligence agent dived headlong into a sexo-emotional tizz directly a likely chip flapped her minky eyelashes at him. The theory, like most of those put about by Snobmass, was a dish of stale codswallop. In fact, the average chip paid to inform on an agent through sexual contact was plain whore, the cheapest postage-stamp in any currency, worthless unless the man she hooked was mentally retarded. Consequently men like himself steered clear of proffered chums who might hop out of warm sheets to snoop about for top *biqbashis* of the Egyptian security service and, on the other side, of hostesses like Miss Sholla Cohen whom the Lebanese courts had sent down for twenty years on charges of procuring agents for Israel during everybody-in parties at her apartment. These daughters of Delilah and Rahab lent an oldfashioned atmosphere to contemporary Middle East intrigue but they were few. And then he also doubted if any woman got breathless at beholding his male beauty. The last woman to chase him believing he had money ran off to hunt elsewhere, oh ten years ago. Therefore, yes, the interlude with Nofret Gohar was queer. Her conduct implied something but it was denied by what she had said. She had an unreal line of conversation complicated by the fact that she listened to herself saying dramatic and female things to a man.

He licked his lips. Either the heat or his encounter with Dominis last night had given him a persistent headache ... so without assistance from revelation he had to theorise from available information. He had to be pragmatic. The theory or theories he got ready for Julian Rand must be viable. Yattle was useless.

He went to the wardrobe to switch on his transistor radio. It was tuned to Kol Israel. An old-sounding voice was talking in Hebrew about pogroms in Poland sixty years ago. He dialled to an Egyptian station which was putting out a repeat of a concert by the redoubtable Um Kalthum, her voice full of familiar power. He listened moodily for several moments, switched off, and went for another prowl round the room, listening to buts and ifs bang through his mind like fireworks. His theories amounted to a ton of straws. He had to extract from it something which might help Rand. As this affair shaped, Rand was the last man to handle it. But as Swann himself said, they faced a manpower shortage.

He sat down on the bed and put his hands between his knees and looked bravely at the wallpaper. It didn't take the hint and dissolve. Someone in a too-near bedroom sang happily. At least, he supposed they were happy because they kept straight on doing it. His ears detected notes off-key by European acoustical preferences which brought back a memory of Noël Coward glancing round an orchestra at rehearsal and saying in that voice 'Do I hear a bum note, gentlemen?'

His brain was an ancient dustbin full of questions. They ranged from how the note got into his pocket at Marraqesh to how anybody became wealthy after his family inheritance, if any, was shared between nine full brothers and possibly as many half-brothers and his known income came from selling tourist dolls and running a brothel. Amer gave an impression of seeking larger rewards than they would provide.

The close heat of the room lay inside his head like a permanent cloud. Two things were clear. Whatever its intention, this plot was on the level. Therefore he must keep out of it. His job was to give Rand something to work on.

Time went by. He dealt himself hands of clock patience. He went for small walks round to revive his circulation. He read a bit of poetry from one of his travelling books. He brushed his teeth. He lay on the floor and did press-ups. And he was unaware of the hours passing until darkness shut down outside the window with the finality of a theatre curtain coming down on a failed play, the shrouding rag.

He got up stretching his arms as he went across to switch on the light. The sudden glare stung his eyes. He glanced at his watch. Though he had lost his appetite it was time for a meal. He washed and dug out another shirt and unearthed a tie and gave it a Windsor knot. He performed each task mechanically, his mind probing at his thoughts. After each chore he had to glance at the mirror to be sure he had done it. He decided to take a book along to share his meal, choosing Michael Astor's *Tribal Feeling*.

At the door he heeled round as always to give the room a careful appraisal and fix the position of everything visible in his mind. He sniffed cautiously. Enshrined was the word.

He swore quietly, went out, and slammed the door. As he went down the corridor the man next door started to pray.

Towards the end of his dinner at one of the Arab restaurants near Herod's Gate he glanced round at the other diners. The restaurant was full. Most people were Europeans, mainly greyhaired men and women indifferent to the perils of 'foreign food'. At one table four woolly-haired African priests giggled frequently. Nearby a youngish nun who had kept her skin pale and coldlooking despite the constant midsummer heat held animated conversation with a middleaged couple and two stylishly-clad women who might be her parents and sisters. Near the entrance sat a solitary woman whose heavily-lidded eyes stared fixedly from her beautiful sour face. There were several new-style city Arabs, wealthy businessmen of one variety or another, grey of suit, white of shirt, twentieth-century cosmopolites by outward appearance. Three were accompanied by women. If the silence at their table was evidence, the three women were wives.

Nobody heeded him. Whenever he had noted who came in or went out he saw that other people were giving their attention to their companions or their plates. It meant nothing. One or other might be on his tail. Outside someone might be getting hungry.

He drank another cup of thick black coffee while he thought about Nofret Gohar. At this distance he was getting her into clear perspective. It became increasingly interesting.

He went back to his book.

When he left the restaurant his fidgety mind had evolved several theories. They were probably wrong but they were something. He hoped so. The thing might balloon to frightening dimensions.

He got to his hotel without seeing signs of anyone following him. Every single stratagem taught him failed to reveal another shadow sewn onto his heels.

The small lobby was empty save for the receptionist hovering around his desk like an acolyte.

He went over to the staircase and ran up it two steps on each stride, swung down the corridor to his room, and opened the door. For an instant he thought he must have left on the light. Then his mind cleared as he saw the girl he met in Sabri's bedroom; she had a knack for getting into bedrooms. She stood beside the window watching him. On the foot of the bed was her large handbag. Her right hand held the baby automatic as if it was a lily. She smiled friendlily at him.

'Come in,' she said politely. 'Please shut the door, will you?'

10

THE situation was pretty incredible.

He hovered on the verge of sad laughter. His feet had strayed into fantasy. Maybe he had an unknown inbuilt time-machine which had suddenly gone out of control to flip him back to the pre-First World War period. It never did happen like this. It differed in details of profound significance. This ignored every rule. In addition to which she still looked exactly like somebody's young sister affecting to be grown up, 'with it' as the present drab phrase put it, her young face almost childishly blank. She evidently thought her conduct effective if unnormal. Her attitude implied confidence in her ability to shoot him if he became truculent plus certainty that she could then either stay put and explain everything satisfactorily or simply leave without hindrance. Well, yes, the damnedest things did happen. But he doubted her chances.

As he stared at her he was aware of a man and a woman talking enthusiastically in a nearby room while the man next door prayed steadily. Here all was quiet.

'Come in and shut the door,' she repeated a shade sharper and waved the automatic as if she was about to spray roses with it. 'Don't be foolish, Mr. Silk.'

It was really too funny for anyone to take seriously. As a situation it was older than the beard of Methuselah but she continued to disregard essential features.

He disobeyed instructions by leaving the door wide open while he remained in the entrance holding the door-handle. 'Well well well, what a pleasant surprise!' he exclaimed in his friendliest loud voice. 'I was afraid you couldn't come. This cheers up my evening considerably. Why didn't you telephone a message? Is Abdullah here too? I want to see him.' He paused, watching her while he listened. The nearby couple had broken off their conversation and the prayerful man was momentarily quiet, both heedful of the happy male voice greeting a friend. In a swift whisper he said: 'Go and put that thing into your handbag, leave it on the bed, and come here. Sharp!' Without giving her an opportunity to speak he raised his voice again. 'Wouldn't you prefer to go downstairs where we can be comfortable? I always get my bedrooms messy and it's hot here. Shall we go down there?'

His slight gesture directed her attention to the silence. It had the poised quality of people eavesdropping for an answering voice. Her eyelids drew tight. Slowly, reluctantly, she went to the bed and did what he ordered.

He chattered another couple of welcoming sentences. She moistened her lips. Then she came towards him with the happiness of someone about to climb the scaffold as the main character in a little drama. Her tailor-made was charcoal grey. Her blouse and shoes were black. He saw two rings on her lovely hands which he would have sworn were absent last night. Despite everything she still reminded him of the girl next door back home. He shunned neighbourliness; her retreat into obedience was without guarantee of continuing compliance. As she halted a pace away he watched her steadily. The door behind him was wide open.

'I take it this is an attempt at blackmail,' he said quietly. 'You start a rumpus unless you get money.'

She smiled the tiniest smile ever born. 'Must you pretend to be a fool?' she asked gently.

He ignored the question. 'I thought there was something strange about you last night,' he said. 'You must have broken into Sabri's room to blackmail him too. Now listen to me, young woman. I'll give you five minutes to get out of this hotel provided you promise to stay clear of me. I loathe being bothered by petty blackmailers. I'll give you this one chance to think over what this filthy business means. At your age——'

'Stop acting,' she said gently. 'The role of oldfashioned British moralist doesn't suit you.'

'Five minutes. You can pick up your handbag at the desk tomorrow morning.'

'We want your help.'

He widened his eyes. 'You expect to get it by brandishing a gun at me?' he asked incredulously.

'I thought you might be someone else.'

'Who would want to break into my room?'

'Several people are curious about you.'

They were speaking rapidly, their voices parrying each other like swords wrapped in cottonwool, both of them listening to sounds coming from other parts of the hotel. From next door came the familiar mumbling drone which rose and fell on queer inflexions. Farther off the plumbing was grumbling like a healthy young camel re-enjoying the meal it had four days ago.

'Why?' he asked.

'I don't know.'

'This is absurd.'

'It's true.'

'Four minutes.'

She gave him what used to be called a calculating stare. 'You are Dorian Silk,' she said softly. 'You were what the British call a public-schoolboy and went to university. You failed as an actor. You were one of the husbands of an actress whose paternal name I have forgotten. Her given name is Gillian. I've seen photographs of her. She is very beautiful.'

'Thank you. I'll tell her.'

'Do you see her?'

'We send each other dirty postcards. Three minutes.'

'You are a failure. You toured America from coast to coast for two years doing various jobs. You wrote two plays.

Both of them failed. You wrote two excellent books, one about this area, the other about North Africa, and your prophecies have come true. Your psychological attitude has prevented you from having literary success. You ran a tourist company out here which failed. Hardly any newspapers use the news agency you work for now.'

She was making it much easier for him. 'Why are you telling me this?' he asked.

'I want you to realise I know about you so you will let me talk to you.'

'What about?'

'Please shut the door. I promise you I will behave.'

'That,' he said coldly, 'is hard to believe. Very well, I'll hear what you want to say. Go back to the window—no, don't turn, walk backward. It's directly behind you, about six or seven steps.'

As she retreated he went across to the bed, picked up her handbag and opened it, got out the automatic, put down her bag and stepped back to the doorway, his gaze on her throughout.

'Well?'

'Close the door.'

He leant his back against the wall. In his loud friendly voice he said: 'Well, we'd better leave the door open, it's stuffy in here.'

She gazed at him as if she thought that she might discover a chink which would reveal what thoughts sidled or blundered through the grey matter of his brains. He saw tension go from her lips.

In a weak voice she said: 'I'll help you if you help us.'

'How?'

'Sabri wants to see you,' she said. The announcement came from her lips like a string of carefully cultured pearls. 'He will give you an exclusive story.'

'Why me if I'm such an almighty failure at everything I do?'

'I told him about your books. He seldom reads books.'

He nodded approval at a deft wifely touch. The Arab maxim 'Every woman leads to a man' might prove true but he doubted that she was wife to any man. Against his better judgment, against every reason he had given himself on the necessity to steer clear of this thing, he was intrigued. That was completely wrong. But it was him. And he had reasons. Headed by the ineffectual Rand.

'I don't understand this,' he said bluntly. 'If you've got a worthwhile story—if—then according to your opinion of me and my lousy professional connexions it should go to someone who can ensure it has adequate coverage. There are other points. If you came to offer me this story, why threaten me? That sticks in my gullet. More importantly, what's the story?'

She continued to appear childishly naive. Her natural eyebrows drew together in a natural sort of frown. 'He will tell you what it is,' she said and hurried on: 'I find such affairs too complex to understand. He is very clever about them. I chose you because I've read your books. I believe you can handle the story he will tell you better than ordinary reporters due to your comprehension of people here. At first he refused to see you. I persuaded him we must have you or someone like you to help us. You have the ability to treat this properly. Finally he accepted my opinion. Please help me,' she begged pleadingly. 'I had great difficulty in getting him to agree.'

He stared at her with the keen wise eyes of a Man of Destiny. The performance was unlikely to win theatrical awards but it was based on keen wise stares by Men of Destiny who gazed significantly at television cameras for a few years before you forgot their names and wondered whatever had become of them since. Evidently his performance was adequate. She watched him anxiously, hopefully, youthfully, femalely, sure he had fallen for that load of rubbish. She was a bland little liar. But he was curious.

After a significant pause he said: 'How much money does he want for this story?'

'We haven't discussed money.'

'Do you take me for a fool? Everybody who has an exclusive story worth print wants money for it. You must have talked about it.'

'He will take my advice.'

'Are you his business manager too?'

'He knows I am better at business than he is.'

'Does he? Good for him. Women drive a harder financial bargain than men. They always go for the highest price.'

'Of course,' she agreed as if faintly surprised. 'I realise you lack the money which big newspapers can pay. But you can sell this story to big newspapers. It will make a lot of money. You and I can discuss a contract on our way and we'll write it out.'

'That will be to my disadvantage if there are heavy extra expenses.'

'I said we can discuss terms.'

After another pause he said: 'Very well, we'll go back to that crummy joint.'

'Oh, we left it this morning,' she said in a frank tone.

He watched her but nothing about her suppliant manner gave her away as an adroit liar. Oh, she was adroit. Her candid eyes, her youthful face, her deep voice, would have fooled anyone who had failed to check on Sabri. She was either badly trained or careless or desperate. While they looked at each other he rubbed his forehead. He was aware that this was probably the point of no return. At this stage he could still back out, wash his hands of it, leave it to Rand. He could be unlike himself.

'Where is he?' he demanded abruptly.

'He has gone into hiding.'

'Where?'

She began to speak, then fell silent at the approach of voices. A man and a woman came upstairs talking cheerfully over what they had done since afternoon. She raised her brows disdainfully at the finger he pointed at her, warning her to keep quiet. The man and woman went past in a gale of laughter; maybe they could get by without squabbles tonight. Their door slammed shut.

'Well?' he said.

'We thought it best to go to a house outside of the city.'

'How far is it?'

'A mile. I have a car.'

'Who is driving it?'

'I drove it here but you can drive if you prefer it.'

'What is his business?'

'He will tell you.'

This was not his brightest evening. She had given her answers quicker than he could think up questions or switch the line of interrogation while trying to get basic information. At the latter she had come out on top. Without indication or fluster she had left everything of importance till later. Nonetheless, he was a sucker once he got to sniffing at a case. And whatever her unrevealed purpose she had courage. Irritably, cursing himself for being the world's prize muggins, sure he would regret it, he gave in. It would help Rand, he told himself.

'Oh, very well,' he said sourly. 'How long will it take?'

'You may want to talk for some while,' she answered and her voice sharpened as he took his back off the wall. 'Wait. Do you promise wide reportage for what he tells you?'

'I'm modern.'

'What does that mean?'

'I worship money,' he said and stretched his arms. 'It's been a long time since I saw a green sea of it. You give me a worthwhile story. I'll get the lolly for us.'

She damn nearly sneered. 'You're very shiftless, aren't you?' she said. 'What a pity.'

'I shall end up looking exactly like everyone else I bet you,' he said and turned into the open doorway. 'Wait here.'

'Where are you going?' she demanded angrily.

He turned back to face her. 'You're a big married girl so I'll tell you,' he said in a confidential tone. 'At the end of this corridor is a dear little bathroom with other novelties too. You say we may talk for quite a while. So I'm going down to the dear little bathroom and I shall occupy it for thirtyfive seconds. Are you worried? Would you prefer to come with me and hold my hand?' He turned away out of the room.

She had parked the car a hundred yards down the road. It was one of those vehicles you inhabited for six months before you chanced on the family of four which had camped snugly in one corner of the rear since it was built around them on their tour of the assembly line. Its long sleek body was the blue of sapphires. Inside were acres of demure grey upholstery. The seats supported you with the reverential solicitude of old family retainers. Only a pilot's licence would qualify the driver for manipulating the massed gadgets glowing along the instrument panel. It had a left-hand drive. As glittery status symbols went it was pretty impressive but calculated to cause high blood pressure if you wanted to park it in any city in a hurry.

He handed her into it politely. Then he went for the long trot round to the door beside the driving-seat. By the moment he got there he felt winded. It was pleasant to sit down behind the wheel to gaze at every shining dial intended to make driving more stylishly intricate.

While he familiarised himself with the gadgetry the girl said: 'Mr. Silk.' He turned and peered at her. She sat some distance off but he saw the new automatic held in her right hand which was pointed directly at him. 'Do you see this?' she asked gravely. 'You are not very clever, Mr. Silk. You will be wise to do exactly what I say.'

He glared at her. 'You little bitch,' he said sullenly.

11

ON INSTRUCTIONS from the girl he drove south past the shadowy Garden of Gethsemane. Cars full of ageing tourists overtook them en route for the hotel on the Mount of Scandal. An occasional weary old country bus staggered sleepily into the city. At another quiet direction he turned onto the main road which looped east at the start of the journey to the capital city Amman.

He maintained his air of sullen compliance. His companion sat trimly composed well out of reach, giving an atmosphere of having complete command of the situation. Pale dashboard light showed her three-quarter face pensive with thought, another faint smile on her lips, her body relaxed. Her right hand was out of sight beside her hips. As it held the automatic her precaution had sense.

Away from the city, tilting down through hills to the Jordan valley, the heat began to rise. Their headlights picked up people straggling back to their villages, several of them on horseback and others on meekly trotting donkeys. Scattered tinselly stars gave the sky a cheap fairground shine.

'Where are we going?' he asked finally.

'You need only follow my instructions.'

'I'll breathe too, thanks. Is it Amman?'

She ignored the question.

'For Heaven's sake, be reasonable,' he said angrily.

'We shall reach our destination safely if you do what I say.'

'Must I explain it? If we have a long journey ahead of us

we should reduce fatigue caused by tension. Nervous stress is accumulative. There's every reason why we should reach the end of the journey fresh. I'm scarcely likely to kidnap you. If you and I were the last man and woman alive we would avoid each other. So I'm unlikely to bother you now. Schoolgirl brides with guns are without charm for me.'

Her profile remained expressionless though she did let her head dip slightly to acknowledge that her ears were working.

The car drifted down through the night at eighty miles an hour.

He let several miles die away. Then he said: 'You've overlooked another point which may have considerable effect on our situation.'

'What is it?'

'This go-kart,' he said mildly. 'Would you call it anonymous? It might be elsewhere but cars are still memorable here, certainly those of this size. Do you imagine people will forget it even at night? We're flinging up dust like a plane laying vapour trails. You tell me Sabri has enemies. If they followed him and yourself to his hideout, they may now be following us. Consequently we may be creating trouble for ourselves by your refusal to tell me where we are going. That prevents me from taking evasive action to throw them off our trail. If you expect big friendly hugs and ham sandwiches when we get there, you may be wrong. That being so, there is this matter of timing our journey. Should we get there fast? Should we choose an hour to get there? The way you're playing it we will arrive in a fine old state of strain, you from playing guard over me, me from being completely in the dark about your reasons for taking me there at gun-point. What's the point if we get there to find your husband dead?'

It was cruel but she was doing everything wrong.

Along the next straight stretch of road he glanced at her. She had turned her head to look at him. From what he could tell her eyes were a darn sight emptier than the sky.

She averted her gaze and her shoulders shifted uneasily.

'Is it fair to frighten me now?' she asked blankly.

'Why should I get nervous alone?'

'Do you imagine I'm ignorant of the dangers?'

'You act like it,' he told her. 'If you are scared, where's the harm in my putting it into words? You float into my room like a fairy. You order my assistance at gun-point. You trick me when I've showed willing to assist you. Now you want me to believe I'm simply your chauffeur. Oh, you probably think you're handling this situation superbly. Wrong, sweetie, you're doing an incredibly bad job. How can I help you willingly like this? There are pleasanter occupations.'

'Women,' she said contemptuously.

'Gorgeous if human.'

The valley heat rose steadily. He switched on the air cooler but even though they kept the windows almost closed he felt sweat trickling down his chest and gathering around his loins. Here, close to the north shore of the Dead Sea, they were far down on the earth's surface. Heat gathered around them like clouds. The wheel was slimy under his hands.

At length she said: 'We are not going to Amman.'

'Oh good! Well, there are several other places. Peking perhaps? Or Buenos Aires? Or—let me guess—Helsinki?'

'Do you like schoolboy humour?'

'I always adapt myself to my company.'

'Oh, very well,' she sighed. 'He's hiding near Ma'an.'

'Holy grief!'

Her laugh hung above their heads while their mobile cell spun deeper into heat. It had the chime of a cracked bell.

'Are you afraid of long night drives?' she asked mockingly. 'We can get there in less than five hours if you are a good driver.'

He thought for a moment. Then he loosened his tie and collar. 'You might have warned me,' he commented.

'And have you walk out on me?'

'I haven't had much chance.'

'You would have found some means. Shiftless men must be resourceful to pay their bills and you are shiftless, Mr. Silk.'

He switched off the cooler. 'Ah, you're right,' he admitted.

'Did hard work ever appeal to you?'

'I'm a fully paid-up trade unionist,' he said defiantly and half-lowered the window beside him.

'You should have employed your abilities,' she told him severely.

'Here endeth the fourteenth lesson,' he said and kept his voice down to an even burr: 'You should run a correspondence college on how to become a success. Five simple lessons, deposit refunded if you fail to triple your income within six months. Let me warn you. This carping emotional tinge you give everything will tire you. Still, play it your style. Mine not to reason why.'

'Sabri will tell you everything,' she said and her voice had reverted to its earlier stoicism.

He judged this the moment to use silence. Inside the car the heat was rising steadily. He began to reduce speed.

Here they were down inside one of the lowest and hottest sections of this crease in the earth's crust which stretched hundreds of miles south to become the Great Rift Valley. Out of the darkness an ancient open flivver came towards them. On it two dusty-robed Jordanians joggled stiffly like wax figures. They had yanked their *qeffiyahs* protectively over their mouths and nostrils to save them the worst of the dust thrown up by the car. This region was empty of horsemen and pedestrians. Local people knew better than to venture into this bleak depression on hot midsummer nights. It was one of those regions which gave rise to grim rumours and superstitions among travellers.

He started to yawn voluptuously. A score of *wadis* flowed into the Jordan from surrounding hills during the brief rains, all the way north to the Sea of Galilee, but they were devoid of cooler air currents always and were nonexistent during summer. Even though the sun had been gone for hours the stale heat seemed to pour clouds of steam into your mind.

He yawned noisily. With an effort he distracted his attention by remembering an evening when he stood on the platform of Kimberley station watching the South African sun—or should it now be the Afrikaner sun?—drop like a melting orange fruit-drop to the veld and directly it had vanished beyond the dusty attic of South West Africa the night pinning down on diamond mines and anthills and high veld turned shivery cold. Here the heat had scarcely diminished since the fruit-drop flew out of sight. It smelled as fragrant as an army dump of old boots fresh from a long route march.

As they drove across the shrunken Jordan, an ooze like black treacle, he yawned again. He was glad he had taken one of his wakey-wakey pills, his main purpose in having left her briefly at the hotel, or this heat would have put him to sleep. Every surface he touched was hot, the wheel close to floating in his sweat, his shirt and pants sticking to his skin. It was one of those occasions when nudity alone was hygienic and sane.

He drove round the curve of the road heading towards the ruins of Tulailat al-Ghassul. When he yawned again muttering propaganda resentment his companion gave her first sign of human frailty. She sought to conceal a yawn by saying: 'You must regret being out of Britain during the Shakespeare quatercentenary celebrations.'

He seized on the chance like a man trying to forget his tiredness. 'My dear young woman,' he said icily, 'may I remind you that it was also the quatercentenary of Kit Marlowe and it is to the eternal discredit of Britain that the event was almost ignored. Consider the insult. Marlowe's poetry provided the model for Shakespeare. Our Willie pinched hundreds of lines from Marlowe and changed only a few words in them. Marlowe's *Edward II* set the dramatic formula for all of Shakespeare's histories. His *Jew of Malta* and *Tamburlaine* were the mould for most of Shakespeare's other plays. His *Faustus* influenced Goethe and other European writers. He did the hard literary work for Shakespeare and others. And at least he justified the personal weaknesses of homosexuality and drunkenness attributed to him though he was too deeply involved in politics for the truth about his personal character to be clear. State papers and so on have often been altered to discredit someone. The latest biography of Marlowe, by Professor Rowse, has not cleared up the mysteries involving Marlowe. However, I will agree that Marlowe was not responsible for the plays of Shakespeare.'

'You sound like one of those angry young men playwrights.'

'My dear woman,' he said exasperatedly, 'the last thing those young men were was angry. They merely dug up squalid personal relationships among poor unstable sections of the British community to break from other dramatic themes. It was their gimmick. But it wasn't new. George Bernard Shaw said the same things seventy years ago. The dramatic mould for the so-called angry young men was Walter Greenwood's *Love on the Dole*. But angry? One small pooh. It was their entrance. One or two may keep on writing. The others are already forgotten names. Three or four have become lardy middleaged businessmen living in porridgy houses on the fringe of faceless suburbs and playing the stock markets. Occasionally they open literary chats as The Distinguished Literary Personality Mr. Um Pah. You should use your intelligence instead of swallowing fashionable judgments. Even the judges are dubious.'

Thoughtfully, over another yawn, she said: 'You obviously dislike women intensely. Your wife must be responsible.'

He failed to see what attack of female logic produced that decision. 'Wrong,' he assured her. 'I fall for marvellous sleek wild women who've fresh ideas about old sins. If that is possible.'

She changed the subject. 'Can you get to Ma'an in five hours?' she asked and checked another yawn.

'We,' he reminded her, 'we.'

'Can you?'

'I suppose so,' he agreed sourly. 'Would it be better to wait till daylight?'

'No. Are you still in love with her?'

'Who?'

'Your ex-wife.'

'You're imprecise, Mrs. Sabri. Gillian is nobody's ex-wife. Speech-wise, to borrow a hackneyed modern term, this is a pretty battered century but the word wife has historical implications if nothing else. For your information as you're interested in what were my private affairs, she is a victim of circumstances. Nobody has provided a respectable alternative to marriage. Terribly keen on respectability, Gillian. Does that satisfy you?'

'You're candid about her.'

'Can I deny headlines about her and my husbands-in-law?'

'You came here to forget her.'

'You sweet oldfashioned thing. I'm another fugitive from the British climate and politicians.'

She yawned candidly and settled more comfortably into her corner. 'She must be very attractive,' she said.

'True.'

'Why did you marry her?'

' "Pooh, my dear, any port in a storm," as the sailor said to Fanny Hill.'

'Your life with her gave you opportunities to be successful which you haven't gotten now,' she said schoolmarmishly.

He grunted. This hunger for trivial chat had been her first indication of weakness. It might mean what he hoped; that for unexplainable reasons she had failed to take a wakey-wakey pill and was afraid of heat and the monotony of night travel tiring her.

He switched his line of attack. She talked casually, desultorily, but he merely mumbled occasionally, praying that his earlier stream of words followed by this switch would achieve what he wanted.

As he took the car slowly up through weird layers of heat he caught sight of a battered tangerine sort of moon sliding among hills. Its ochrous sheen failed to improve this landscape of quarter-light broken by queer oblique patches of shadow. Miles away a Bedu campfire licked at the darkness like a kitten's tongue dabbing at its fur. There were enough stars to keep astronomers twittering till dawn.

Gradually her voice stumbled into silence. Eventually she stopped talking. He glanced at her and saw that her eyes were shut. He muttered aimlessly. Driving one-handed he got out his handkerchief. Then he picked the capsule from the breast-pocket of his jacket to where he had transferred it from one of the several small pockets in his trousers while he was in the hotel bathroom. He put it into the handkerchief and interrupted his mumble twice to hold his breath. His companion did not speak. He inhaled deeply, broke the capsule, and instantly stretched out his arm to hold the handkerchief close to her face. At the same time he held his breath and slowed the car. The girl's head fell forward. He stopped the car. He kept the handkerchief close to her face. She drooped sideways towards him. At once he opened the door and got out, gulping air into his lungs. He threw the handkerchief away.

The heat was like an invisible feather-bed which adjusted itself against him. He reached into the car and switched off the headlights and heeled round studying the darkness. Under the tawdry stars the land was devoid of even the slightest glimmer of light from car or house. He saw wide ragged patches of shadow formed by hills broken by dribbles of ochrous pallor which slopped down ridges or gathered like curdled cream at the bottom of dents which resembled the impress of large thumbprints. The night was so soundless he could almost hear the splash of sweat bouncing down his ribs and streaming inside his thighs.

He circled his arms lazily to ease his stiff shoulders. In this dark solitude he and his unconscious companion might be the last Canaanites escaping from ancient disaster or fleeing from primordial holocaust. Absence of adequate light, and stillness, and landscape, heightened the illusion.

He cleared his mind to act logically. Errors at this stage might produce endless complications later.

Taking another glance at the night he went round the car and opened the door beside the girl. She was motionless, her body slumped away from him, her head fallen towards her farthest shoulder. He took the automatic from her limp hand, snicked on its safety-catch, slipped it into the left-hand pocket of his jacket, took off his jacket and laid it on top of the car. Her huge handbag contained enough odds and ends to launch a jumble sale. Plus another clip of bullets and a dinky little torch. He put them into his pockets.

As he wiped the palms of his hands on the seat of his trousers a small spurt of light attracted his attention. It was a shooting star on its headlong rush to join red giants and blue dwarfs poised at the verge of infinity.

He watched it vanish from sight. Nothing else warranted his interest. He bent low inside the car. His attempt to haul the girl out caused her to fall back along the seat, her legs sliding weakly towards him. That alarmed him lest the capsule had done something unexpected. He knelt on the floor to undo her blouse and ease his hand under the most unArab bra he had seen for years. He gave a small hiss of relief. If anything her heart beat a darn sight more steadily than his own at present; in about a couple of hours she would wake up feeling fine but slightly dim. Slowly, cautiously, he slid one arm under her thighs and the other beneath her shoulders.

'Come on, gently does it,' he said and lifted her up. She weighed even less than he had expected. He laid her carefully on the ground. Just to be sure, he put his hand over her heart again. It was still beating strongly. Unconsciousness had smoothed her face. She looked about fifteen. Except for her lips. By some odd transmutation darn near alchemy they had a full mature sensuous softness wholly unlike their neatness at hours when she had control of her face. He turned her head sideways to study her profile carefully. He crouched on his heels gazing at her in the light of the small torch thinking his thoughts. Then he set to work.

He searched her as obsessively as a cartographer recording an uncharted coastline. True enough in one sense. She was a physically trim girl, very nicely put together. His fingers felt pills and capsules hidden inside the handier linings of her clothes. Their location was rather obvious. He left them alone. There was nothing unusual about her handbag because he had expected to find a sort of knife concealed inside one bar of its frame. He pressed it back into its sheath and heard the faint double click of catches which held it secure. To be safe he drew it out again and put it into his left-hand pocket. The contents of her handbag was wholly impersonal, the usual female bric-à-brac. She might be anyone.

'You're careless, chum,' he told her and had another look at her face. He sighed. The Fates were determined to lumber him with those who might be called near-lame dogs. In Iran, the unspeakable Woolf. In Afghanistan, Shamz . . . his lovely Shamz who would have crowned him if he had let her guess at the thought. In Azerbaijan, Tanya, the scruffiest and most beguiling cat he ever saw. Now this one. He ran a gentle finger down her profile. Well, they had to start somewhere if they were going to start at all. He got to his feet and scratched his forehead. It was apples to doughnuts she carried the vital information inside her young head.

While he searched the car the summer lightning of distant headlights flickering across the darkness above the road from Amman. Moving swiftly he lifted the girl into the car and shut the door, took his jacket off the roof, ran round and climbed in, threw his jacket into the back, and drove a short distance off the road. When the car raced past on its way to Jerusalem the girl and he were curled up apparently asleep though his automatic was already sweaty in his hand.

Directly the car had gone he picked up his jacket and opened the door to lay it on the ground. Then he resumed his search.

He could have spared himself the effort. There was nothing of importance. His haul amounted to two cans of petrol stacked in the boot, a first-aid kit on the floor at the back and a large silver flask beside it containing what smelled like brandy. As he screwed the cap back on the flask he supposed his failure to discover one clue about her provided a modicum of success. Every woman carried around the impedimenta of her identity or personality. Every ordinary woman. His companion chose total anonymity. She was just an oldfashioned girl who believed women should retain mystery. Tra-la. It was unwise of her. He laid the flask down beside the first-aid kit, and shut the rear door. Although the night was still pretty hot he put on the jacket rather than have the possible complication of having to fight for return of its small arsenal.

He settled into the driving-seat and leaned over and tapped her cheek. There was no response. Her eyelids were motionless. She breathed gently and steadily. 'Well, at least you didn't sprinkle wrong information about,' he said. 'Now it depends on what we dig up together.'

He backed the car onto the road, then drove on towards Amman. While she lay motionless against the back of her seat he hummed tunelessly to himself. Once he glanced at her. She was sound asleep, her lips slightly parted.

12

SEVENTYSIX minutes later, dead on the dot, his anonymous companion started to come out of it. His first intimation came with the straightening of her body. He glanced at his watch to check how long the capsule fumes had been effective and thought modern science just wonderful. Soon afterwards her hands fidgeted limply like someone finding out what would function after the party last night.

They had turned southeast across country to join the new desert highway through Al Jizah, the road winding among bleak hill formations overlooking the old railway. He had gone like a rocket to get back lost time. Since he passed horsemen just over half an hour ago the road had been empty of other traffic. He drove on his headlights to have an opportunity to chew things over in his mind while he maintained speed.

The smell of salty dust licked in at him while miles and minutes fell away behind them along the starlit road. At every turn the land was formless, just a waste backed by dark hills of little significance upon the sky. There was less heat up here, just occasional patches broken by others which were so cool they felt cold. His companion snuffled sleepily. There was an interval of featureless miles before she stretched her legs experimentally and eased her head on her neck. Her hands fell off her lap on either side, an action which was singularly unsimple though she did her present best to let it appear natural. He let silence stretch on till he imagined she could think clearer.

He coughed politely. 'If you're wondering what's happened

to your gun,' he said, 'I've got it. Do you hear? I've got your second gun. I've also got the stiletto from your handbag. I have your stiletto. You'd be foolish to be reckless. We're travelling fast. If you doubt me look out of the window. If you act stupidly we may easily finish up dead. Worse, we might finish wishing we had died. Do you hear me?'

She yawned. 'I'm not afraid of death,' she said and managed to push contempt into her voice.

'So I gather. However, if you are reckless we may become disfigured. Be realistic.'

After a pause she sat up and said bitterly: 'I went to sleep.'

'People do. You'll soon feel better for it.'

'Where are we?'

'I've answered that. You wanted to go to Ma'an. We're going there. If my guess is right we'll reach Al Qatranah pretty soon. Who is Dominis?'

He was aware of her head turning towards him. 'Who?' she asked blankly.

'David Dominis, citizen of Washington, D.C. So he told me. He and I had a sort of brawl after I left you at the Isis. As you've been in America, you've probably met him.'

She checked an indrawn breath. 'I've never been to America,' she denied and gave her trembly yawn an affectation of indifference. 'Whatever gave you such an idea?'

He negotiated a succession of curves without slackening speed. The headlights flicked over the grey-white skeleton of an old camel near a dry *wadi*. Over on their left hills rose sharply and swept off in a wide curve. Farther off on their right another range shouldered the lowest stars. He avoided stony patches of worn road.

'You're a liar,' he told her. 'You've lived in America.'

'I've never been there!'

'You're a bigger liar. You are not Mrs. Sabri. You either

know or guess where he is. He never told you he wanted to meet me. If he had the sort of story you told me he has you'd've got onto one of the local reporters for the larger American and European papers or newsagencies to sell it for big cash. You'd have needed immediate money to get both of you away from here. My guess is you know where he is, want information from him and expect me to get it for you. Me—because you haven't anyone else you can call on rightaway. Simultaneously you expect to learn why I wanted to see him when I found you searching his room. Right?'

'You're full of cute theories,' she snapped savagely.

'Listen to that,' he said. 'Here's a woman who has been asleep for nearly two hours, who hasn't got her full waking brain, and who doesn't realize it's dangerous to speak too quickly although she's done her best to persuade me she learned English at a mission-school or something similar. Curious, isn't it? What can we do with her? Maybe she is just a nit, pretty, brave, but a nit. Pity.' Then he said: 'You're frequently careless. I'd like to believe it's because you're rushed and bothered. "Cute theory" was one sample. "Gotten" is another. There have been others. Too many. Courage is not enough. You must do your homework.'

Perhaps it was cruel. Suddenly she saw herself being stripped, shown up as incomplete, her mind sown with instant blooming doubts of her ability. He understood part of what she felt because there are instinctive vocational sympathies between agents. He was pretty sure she was an agent, probably a novitiate on her first solo assignment though that left several things unsaid. If his theory was right, well, everyone had to start somewhere even on a tough assignment. It was on the cards she might do something desperate to revive her self-confidence. Women were guided, or otherwise, by devious logic. She might wait for a situation which she believed she could turn to her advantage.

'Well?' he demanded.

She was silent.

When he glanced at her the dashboard lights illuminated her masklike face. She had drawn away and sat sideways in the right angle formed by the door and the back of the seat. Her lean young face, the pale glow on her wide cheekbones and long neck, reminded him of the famous bust of the ancient Egyptian queen Nefertiti. He wondered if the similarity gave her a private giggle sometimes. Her lowered lids shone above the black fringes of her eyelashes. Her hands lay limp on her lap.

'You'd better answer my questions,' he warned menacingly. 'Who was the Chinese who went to Sabri's room after I left you?'

'I don't know.'

He laughed shortly. 'Let's understand each other,' he said. 'We're a long distance from where you could scream hopefully. Ears are absent. You thought I was a pushover to do your dirty work. There is dirty work coming. I can smell it. Meanwhile we're alone and it's a dark night. Every labourer is worth his hire. Even me. Suppose we stop for a little payment on account?'

'Must you talk like a tv script?'

'You've only yourself to blame for how I talk, Miss— Miss What?'

'I told you who I am.'

'You told me lies. One day you may be one of those wives ready to sacrifice all for love but it's in the future. Right now you're just another girl relying on guns.'

Her faint sigh indicated indifference.

He drove through the darkened huddle of houses which was Al Qatranah, past a pencil-thin manarat, and increased speed on the road to Unaizah. This section of road showed signs of recent renovations to accommodate tourist traffic en route to Petra, the 'rose-red city half as old as time'. Apart from their headlight wands the only light was that bouncing wearily off the shabby tangerine and the dime-store lustres littering the sky. A warm air was coming towards them from the south.

He let her think till they were crossing open country.

'Stop deluding yourself,' he warned her. 'We are alone. Look round if you doubt me. I have your weapons and you have a story, you tell me. Unless we combine those factors we might as well stop here and go back directly it's light. You must stop fooling around . . . for example, Sabri must be an odd Arab to let his wife dress up nights to wander round the streets for low-income customers. Ah!' he jeered at her sudden hiss, 'good. Contact! Let's begin there. You thought your local colour costume an adequate disguise for my bleary eyes. Wrong. I saw just sufficient of your face under the wig. By pure chance you have very striking looks, memorable, very pleasant in an immature sort of style. But clad local style you look much older. Now will you talk honestly?'

She kept silent.

'Okay,' he said at length. 'So let's theorise from there. You saw me while you were prowling near the Dung Gate hoping to meet Sabri. Later on someone told you he was at the Isis. You went there. He was absent but I nosed into the party. You recognised me because you had taken risks to see what I looked like. My arrival proved I was searching for him. Logic says you would have almost forgotten me if you located him easily. Right? Now the guesses. One, either your previous informant or somebody else told you where you can find Sabri. Two, you believe it may be dicey to get to him . . . if you could reach him easily you would be travelling alone because fatigue would not matter if you expected a friendly welcome. Three, you decide to kill two birds with one stone. I provide extra protection and may be persuaded to tell you why I want to see him. Neat. Brave. But slightly desperate, I think. Let's go on a bit. Four, if you are a Jordanian why should you do this job when there are loads of policemen available who could jump to his rescue? If policemen can do the job, why should you get me to do it at gun-point? Therefore, you are working apart from the police. It becomes stranger when I wonder why Sabri came back to Jerusalem and suddenly took fright. Anyway, here we are, on our way, you say, to find him. I think your conduct suggests you believe that or you intend to get me somewhere so that I can be killed. But why should anyone want to kill me? That question is academic at present. Meanwhile we are alone. I don't want to rough you up. I dislike roughing women. But it's up to you. If we aren't in business together, then I'm in it for myself. You choose.'

There was a long silence while she communed with her cautions.

'Why do you want to see him?' she asked finally.

'Whatever you think of me and my work, I go after stories. I'm not a bum reporter. My "someone" told me Sabri has a worthwhile story. I agree with you—I need good stories to get back into big-time reporting. I had creditors, notably the tax people. You know how it is. I daren't go on strike. Have you heard how the British love to strike? I just daren't afford to be a rugged individualist about money.'

She maintained a Sphinxlike silence for a couple of miles. When she did speak the words came as if they were wrenched from her. 'What information do you expect to get from him?' she asked.

'I've no idea,' he lied. 'But your conduct and these quick changes of clothes, your various weapons, make me hopeful that it isn't a waste of energy. Most promised scoops are duller than the village pond.' He switched the line of conversation. 'Tell me about Dominis. Who is he? Very American. Five hundred and fortythree percent. American. Overly American.'

'What is he like?'

'The answer to most maidenly prayers. Six feet four. Two hundred and twentyfour pounds if he is an ounce. Grey eyes like balloons. Pale olive skin. Black hair—what is it?'

'Has he big square teeth?'
'You could pave the garden path with 'em.'
'His hair?'
'Helpful if the radio breaks down.'
'Big hands?'
'They could mince a fighting bull.'
Unwillingly she said: 'He has been following me.'
'Even he must have good taste. Why?'
'I don't know.'
He let her contemplate her thoughts.

This section of road needed repair. It slowed them, the tyres throwing up a musical-box tinkle of stones underneath. Over on their left the railway line to the Hijaz stretched straight for mile after mile. The land was without sight of fires or lights. Apart from themselves the region was as still as Bedu travellers had known it for thousands of years.

Reluctantly she said: 'He may assume I know something about Sabri.'

'Oh, you do. How much do you know?'

'Hardly anything.'

He shook his head. 'You insult your own intelligence,' he commented. 'This is an occasion when courage is insufficient. Are you Russian?'

After a pause he glanced at her. She was staring at him. Perhaps it was a mite fanciful to liken her eyes to black flames but less flamboyant similes were meaningless. If she had her wish they would have given him third-degree burns.

'Must you insult me?' she asked, her voice brittle as supermarket giveaway glass tumblers.

He gave his attention to the unreeling road. 'Now that's a damn silly thing to say,' he said amusedly. 'Millions of ordinary decent people are proud of being Russian.'

Her lovely hands jerked impotently.

'Russia is a vulture waiting to tear this region apart.'

'Ah. So you're not Russian and you're not Jordanian. What are you?'

She kept silent.

His efforts to persuade her to talk about herself were unsuccessful. Eventually he gave up to let her imagination fill the silence. It would.

Their headlights carved the night monotonously. Miles farther on they met a car travelling north. He drove through falling skeins of dust for several seconds. As they got clear of the mirk their lights wheeled over two tents and sleeping camels and horses gathered at the roadside; the camels, *Ata Allah*, 'gift of God', were the first he had seen for some days in this land where they were once supreme. Whenever he glanced at his companion her face was as blank as next year's diary.

At quarter-past two they approached Ma'an.

He could think of livelier places to reach at night. Until recently it had been an isolated small town hardly known outside Jordan. Tourism had changed that but could not restore its ancient importance. Here, long before Christ came to instruct and while the deserts were young, generations of Nabataean Arabs over hundreds of years lived and procreated and died in a conviction that they dwelt at the centre of the universe and that their carved-rock capital at Petra, hidden by the long narrow *siq*, the pass winding through towering cliff formations, was eternal. Vestiges of Nabataean belief still existed to greet Roman *caligatae*, booted ones, who trudged down to establish their base at Petra. Directly they withdrew history bypassed the region. Petra was lost to everyone except local Arabs for five hundred years, its magnificent buildings an occasional shelter for groups of Bedu and desert brigands, till a Swiss explorer on a quiet stroll chanced on it accidentally. And if that history wasn't spooky he didn't know what qualified for the description. What happened to Petra could happen to any city.

Now this country was the domain of the Howeitat, one of the most powerful and prideful Bedu tribes though in these years its women seldom cried the *zaghruut* to send their men off on a *ghazu*, raid, of the sort which had made them famous and respected as warriors.

While he thought about tribal wars which had stormed across this ochrous region the girl's voice broke into his contemplations. 'Slow down,' she ordered abruptly. 'We're nearly there. It wouldn't be wise to stop outside the house.'

He reduced speed to a crawl.

Moments later she said: 'Switch off the headlights.'

He did so and asked: 'What are we looking for?'

'The house stands by itself on the left-hand side of the road. First come two houses on the right, about four hundred yards apart. Then there is another house on your side. By itself.'

After a few minutes he said: 'Like that. Now what?'

'Two houses on this side, then another on yours. It is about a quarter of a mile farther on. On your side. It has a high wall.'

Moments later he drove off the road, put the car into reverse and backed onto the road, turning till it faced in the direction they had come. He cut the engine and pocketed the keys. In the darkness he heard her hands rustling over each other to relieve nervous tension.

He licked the corners of his lips. Each tasted as if he had spilled salt into it. 'You get out first,' he told her. 'Wait— wait. For goodness' sake, save your energy. You tire your nerves by rushing. Now pay attention. Leave the door open and take three steps away from it. Directly I get out walk back up the road to restore your circulation. You sit badly, full of tension, and cramp is the last risk we can take. I'll give you two minutes. Thereafter it depends on you. Clear?'

'Let me have a gun,' she pleaded.

'Is it likely? Be careful not to make any noise.'

As she got out he moved onto her seat to shut and lock the door and window. Back on the driving-seat he fastened the window and opened the door. He got out and saw her vanish into the darkness. He locked the door and slid the keys into a small zip-fastened pocket inside the waistband of his trousers. He tested the other doors and wandered about to get his bearings.

On his return she stood waiting for him. She ignored his return, her head raised, studying the cloudless sky. He felt air from the south warm on his face and hands. He could almost smell the sands of Saudi Arabia and that intense stale heat of the Red Sea coming up the Gulf of Aqaba and over the Ash Shefa mountains. Every air which blew over the axe-shaped land of Jordan came from countries around it. So did its political storms. He flicked away sweat trickling into his eyebrows.

She turned slowly to face him. Her eyes were black lightless smudges under their brows. This vague light accentuated angles of her lean cheeks. Her darkly curved lips smiled at him.

'Trust me,' she pleaded. 'Let me have my gun.'

'I don't fancy waking up in the hereafter knowing I had the distinction of being shot in the back by a friend of President Nassah just——'

Her hand flashed up towards his face but fell without completing its journey.

'——to get back at one man from Fleet Street,' he concluded. 'Go ahead. Resist any temptation to play tricks. You'll get a headache or worse.'

She faced him for a long moment before she turned away to go ahead of him. Her composure hardened his suspicions. The soles of her shoes were quiet on the ground. He got her torch out of his pocket and drew his automatic from its holster.

He kept his ears bent on the night ready to pick up the slightest sound. His companion went ahead without hesitation, her confidence telling him she was familiar with the place and had memorised the road surface. He liked how she held herself, the shadowy stir of her hips, her smoothly gliding thighs and legs carrying her with catlike poise and stealth. The darkness spread around them remained silent.

Was it imagination or was there an increase of heat in the air upon his face? It might be tension. He wiped the back of his hands on his jacket.

It took them less than five minutes to reach the house. As its solid darkness took shape upon the stars he realised he was back at his old game of ticking off seconds and minutes to distract his attention. The house stood alone, its roof high above the garden wall, exactly as she had said. Nearing the wall her step faltered and her hands were momentarily restless beside her hips. He lengthened his stride to draw alongside her. Her hand brushed against his. She gave a slight start. It seemed natural. She was unlikely to cause trouble here. He kept close beside her.

Inside shadow cast by the wall he caught hold of her arm. They halted. He listened intently, his gaze prowling around. Across the road were trees, the usual Biblical cluster of cypresses, oily black against the dusty dark blue of sky. To his relief she kept motionless. The sound came again. It did seem to come from the direction of the trees. He was semi-reassured: night birds and bats here did provide quaint squeaks. She went on directly his hand left her.

The gateway was two-thirds along the wall. The gate was solid. It felt warm to his touch but its smoothness was new. She stood quiet. He kept his back to the cypresses opposite and switched on her torch. Its dim glow showed that the gate was off its latch. It swung silently inward at his touch. He put his hand on her shoulder to guide her inside, followed her through, and used his gun hand to push the gate shut. They halted again for him to examine gate, hinges, and adjacent ground. His search failed to discover alarm wires.

She had an intuitive grasp of essentials. Directly his search was over she led him forward. What he could tell of the garden suggested it might be the prize entry of a Japanese sand-garden representing eternity or dishonourable soul on pilgrimage through life. There were two cypresses over on their right. He saw nondescript bushes rising against the left-hand wall of the house. Though they went carefully their shoes found grit at every step.

The house was strictly functional. No one would mistake it for the White House and it boasted less glass than a corporation building. There were just two ordinary windows on either side of a doorway without charm. Upstairs were four other windows.

As they got near to the front door she stopped and turned to him. Her face came up for him to see it. He saw her eyebrows rise, querying his intention. He answered her unspoken question by nodding at the front door. She went on gazing at him. He knew she was pleading to be given her gun but she might as well have hoped to win a football pool. She swung round impatiently.

Three shallow steps led to the front door. At the top he glanced round again. Then he turned to the door. There was hardly any need to waste torchlight on it. At a slight touch of his hand it swung slowly inward. The darkness on the other side was reverential. He grabbed her just as she was about to enter. Holding her close he drew her back off the steps and started round the house. He had a deep horror of open invitations in these conditions.

They had to crouch low under every window. The second window along the left-hand wall was partly open. Those around the corner were shut. At the back another window gaped on the night. The vague starlight showed another and even less cheerful doorway about eight feet farther on.

Immediately they were past the window he drew her close, slung his left arm over her shoulders so that his hand was under the front of her throat. He felt her tremble at the implication of his action. They went on towards the door like lovers whose parting would be full of sorrow.

At the doorway he put his right shoulder against the wall and reached his left foot forward. She gave a soft breath of evident surprise as the door swung inward. At once his wrist was against her neck. Quietness came out at them like a smell. He waited briefly. Unsatisfied, he drew her back and they circled out across the dim garden like dancers. He kept his wrist on her neck till they were past the corner. Directly its pressure eased she inhaled deeply.

Along the third wall every window was shuttered tighter than those at an Italian girls' finishing school. He was positive there were wrongs things here. This combination of abysmal silence and open doors was a bad augury. It gave him premonitions to heed. An agent about to disregard premonitions should consult his nearest grief therapist about the market price of pine nowadays.

They rounded the last corner to the front of the house. He stopped and put his back against the good solid wall and drew her alongside him. To be safe, he laid his hand on her neck while he had a little think. Suddenly, without permission, she turned inward and rose up and kissed him. Her cold lips were excited, flickering on his like lightning. He was sure his beauty was less responsible than atmosphere. She was taut as whipcord, unable to keep her lips steady. He wondered if she would ask him to commit murder like Oscar Wilde's Salome begging her lecherous stepdaddy 'Give me the head of Jokonaan', except that his companion's excitement might be due to intending to deliver his own head to a third party. Her lips clung to his and he felt her fingertips glide down his jaw. He did not let his senses reel. The third moment was sheer indulgence. By then she was quieter. Perhaps she had needed to slacken tension. As her head went away he took his back off the wall.

They went silently to the front door.

Both of them were breathing nicely as they mounted the steps. He held her close while his right foot eased the door back. The house was so still that the blood beating in his ears sounded downright vulgar. Commonsense rather than kindliness prompted him to lead the way across the entrance, drawing her behind him. Across the threshold he put his back against the wall. She did likewise.

They were so close that he felt the tremor which went through her. It was understandable. His nose too could smell the faintly sour, near animal warmth of people on the hot stale air. When nothing erupted at them he urged her forward. As she obeyed his instruction he switched on the torch.

13

THE searching light roved over garish emptiness.

They stood in a hallway which was wider than could be estimated from outside. Its walls were squat, the ceiling less than eight feet from floor level. Walls and ceiling were painted matt-finish crimson. On this side were two narrow coal-black doors. At the far end was another which faced the front door, dimmed by staircase shadow and partly open. Across the hall were black double doors decorated with primitively ornate geometrical designs painted in deep yellow. They were shut. Eight feet farther on the flight of stairs led straight up to the higher floor. Neither stairs nor banister had artistic pretensions deeper than writhing snakelike red shapes painted on their blackness. The hall lacked carpets and furniture but the paintwork appeared fairly new and was smooth to his touch. Hardly any dust had collected on the floor although the front door was open. Walls and ceiling were devoid of light fixtures, even the bogus ones which appeared in places as status-symbols. The head of the stairs appeared to be without occupants.

Around them was nothing except the close smell of people. It was an unpleasant smell. He was sure it was a wrong smell.

He looked round regretting he was lumbered with a companion. This was an occasion for solo effort unless you had as many arms as a Hindu god. With torch in left hand, gun in right, he would have to take risks about her. He glanced at that low ceiling and these squat walls which gave the place a tunnellike quality. His latent claustrophobia skipped about nervously. Immediately he switched off the torch to count ten silently. His companion remained quiet, waiting on his decisions. That was thoughtful of her. From this point on everything was a toss-up. You did your best in pursuit of what appeared logical but was the outcome of necessity rather than prescience or wisdom.

He put his right hand on her shoulder, balancing it on the side of his palm, and pushed her forward through the darkness till his left hand, trailing along the wall, met the first doorway. She stopped directly his hand pressed down on her shoulder.

As he switched on the dimmed torch his personal risk was slightly less than hitherto. She was about half a pace ahead, partly shielding him from stairway and the doors opposite. It took uncommon restraint to ignore frequent temptations to rush but he overcame them. He took another cautionary glance round and took an awkward hold on the doorhandle, put up one small silent cheer as it gave easily, and pushed the door inward with the toe of his left shoe. At once he switched off the torch and let his other hand communicate to her that they should go through the doorway. She did not complicate life for him. Their shoes were noiseless on the floor. Inside the room they went two paces along the wall. Once again she came to a halt at his signal. He thumbed off the safety-catch on his automatic and reached his left arm away from his body. Suddenly the vague light sprang from the torch. It swept across an empty room painted an ugly ochre shade. Once again the ceiling pressed down low, once again the furniture was remarkable by its absence. He turned off the torch and felt her delayed quiver of tension as she relaxed momentarily. Without delay he urged her back through the doorway into the hall and drew the door shut.

They heeled round in complete silence. He had to go behind her in order to be on her left side so that he could go through the same procedure of reaching his left hand away from his body before he let them have another brief assistance from the torch to get their bearings. The hall was as deserted as the gateway to Heaven on an average day. Odd. Very odd. Odder because he was certain there were people near. He switched off the light.

At the direction of his hand they went across the hall towards the double doors. His mind hunted round for pleasant thoughts to break the monotony. There was only one. Her faint perfume was an incongruous reminder of nicer journeys with a woman. As an oldfashioned square about women he had crossed mental fingers that she would behave sensibly. Certainly her present docile obedience was free from error. His outstretched left arm touched the door.

She was motionless while he searched for and found the door-handles. One gave easily. He took a calculated risk by putting himself in front of her. Her hand gave one slight tremble as he drew her through the doorway.

The room was in total darkness. It smelled as stale as a bedroom which had not had a window opened since the death of Queen Victoria. Memory told him that this was the side of the house where every window was tightly shuttered. He groped one foot behind him to shut the door, then drew her a couple of paces along the wall. Once again he held his left hand away from his body. Its light swept around.

They had the room to themselves.

It went the whole length of the house. Whoever had undertaken its décor had a passionate thing about red. The naked walls glowed like eyes misted with blood. The ceiling was scarlet, pressing down like an incandescent steel plate. On some walls were scarlet panels edged with gold. There was a total absence of furniture, and, yet again, everything was so still that he could hear her quiet breathing like the gentle rustle of spring leaves. He switched off the torch.

Her voice was a breath on his ear. 'I'm sure there is someone here,' she said.

'I know.'

'What shall we do?'

'Come on.'

Outside the double doors he went through the monotonous procedure of flashing the light around. Everything was uninterested in them. He switched off the beam and led her across the hall again to the other door on the other side. It opened soundlessly. Air from the window crept over his face like a skeletal hand. He heeled the door shut and drew her two paces away from it. The open window was a dull square surrounded by black. He sniffed at the sour air and flicked on the torch. She drew a sharp breath.

The man sprawled on his back at their feet wasn't playing dead. Two bullets had gone through his head from above his right ear. Their points of exit were an unpleasant sight.

Abruptly the girl wheeled round. She put her hand over her mouth. Soft grating noises came from her throat. He regretted anything which gave their location away to attentive ears but he was unable to do anything about it. Her other hand clawed at his arm for support. He glanced round at another red emptiness. Then he thumbed off the torch and put it into his pocket. He kneaded muscles at the back of her neck. At length she brought up her head. Her hand signalled reassurance. He took the torch from his pocket. He elbowed her aside and switched on the dim light.

At second sight he saw that flies had already arrived, perhaps a dozen, prowling like prospectors over bulletholes and matter seeped onto the floor. Two stood on one of the staring eyes facing each other like impendent boxers and another sauntered out of the open mouth under the filmishly trim moustache and stopped to clear its front legs daintily. Nothing about the battered face of Gohar remotely suggested the aspirant man of distinction. He was just another dead man, every pretension gone, an unwilling passenger on the big ship. His dark suit was grubby and bloodstained. His white collar was a sweaty rag, his tie a dirty string. Abrasions at the corners of his lips suggested he had been cruelly gagged.

As Silk went down the girl crouched on her heels beside him but kept her head turned away from the task of examining the dead man's pockets. Their emptiness left him unsurprised. The only handkerchief was in the breast-pocket, four tiny white triangles spaced like a geometry exercise. There was nothing else. He got up and helped her rise. She stood up reluctantly, her limbs unwilling to obey his need to maintain their previous pace. Though she had control of herself he felt her fingers clench spasmodically on his arm as they left the room.

He went through the same procedure. Then he led her down the narrow passage alongside the staircase to the partly open door which should lead to a kitchen. And as he stepped into it his right foot hit something solid. Immediately he stopped and drew back his foot. Her fingers telegraphed a question. After a pause he reached out his foot and let the point of his shoe fumble along what lay on the floor. He nearly decided he must trust her. At almost the last instant he chose the alternative risk. He ignored the repeated question telegraphed by her fingers. His shoe searched on till it reached what he sought. He balanced himself carefully, lifted his right foot and brought the edge of its heel down sharply on what was beneath. It seemed that his theory was correct. Live men usually respond if you stamp on their fingers.

He stood on the fingers heavily. It gave his theory additional support. When the fingers took a grinding pressure he leaned his face towards her silhouetted head, his lips close to her ears. 'Hang onto yourself,' he whispered. 'There's another one here.'

In the glow of torchlight the dead man had an air of careless rapture, the gay Spartan who preferred floors to beds for his nocturnal rest. He lay on his side, his back to the open door which led to the garden, his legs spread wide like open scissors. Out of sight under his body was his left arm. His right arm was outstretched. He might have partly wakened and be reaching for a companion who shared his sleep. It revealed one of his lifetime fads. He was a ringo. There were three on the short stubby fingers of his groping hand. One boasted a large ruby, another an outsize turquoise. Dried blood covered the skin from knuckles to wrist. His head was bent towards his right shoulder. Above the back of it flies hovered like settling helicopters. There were wide dust patches on the ancient pale grey jacket and trousers and over-bright brown shoes.

The house remained very quiet. Silk heard only their own breath and the buzzing of larger flies chasing their lesser brethren away from the site of mutual interest. He sniffed at the close air. The kitchen was empty of utensils and furniture. He half-turned, listening. The house remained still: you could have heard a fairy tiptoe. At his slight tug the girl sank down beside him.

He shoved the dead man onto his back. As torchlight illuminated his face she gave a sharp hiss. It was a long narrow face, the large thin nose curving down towards lips hidden by a black moustache whose corners curved down to join a glossy pointed short beard. The eyes had been deep-set under eyebrows like dominoes. Above was ugliness, the exit hole of a bullet fired from a gun which must have been held within inches of the back of the head to cause such an aperture. When he was killed he had been upright and, to judge from the mess which had dribbled down his forehead and cheekbones, must have been held up by some means for a while afterwards. At a guess he had spent thirtyfive years on his journey here. He was slightly built, about five foot six in his socks. Every café and *suq* of every Arab city had its familiar score of such men, small-time fixers endlessly busy on various concurrent schemes to raise *baqshesh*, often crooks and dope-peddlers and blackmailers and rabble-rousers who politicians employed to go out and incite the mobs to greater fury when violence raged along the streets. At another guess he had gone aboard the big ship six hours ago. And she recognised him.

He eased back on his heels. This was hardly a moment

for scampering accusations at her. She might need inducements before she was ready to share her knowledge, a matter of time. That gave him one problem. Another was that her reaction should have been different if the man was Sabri. Different and much earlier. She should have recognised the clothes, the rings, the height. But her reaction came only at sight of the face. And her reaction to their sight of Gohar seemed to have been plain revulsion.

He moved quickly but not quickly enough. There was a soft flutter like powder-puffs bashing air and the sudden sour smell of newly distilled sweat. In the semi-darkness the man hit the back of his head a savage blow and grabbed his shoulders. Simultaneously his right wrist was kicked. It jerked open his fingers and the automatic fell on the floor. At once he threw aside the torch rather than risk letting it help the opposition. Strong hands yanked him up. He ought to have bright ideas on how an intrepid agent behaved but coherent thought was too much hard work.

He did his best to grapple with his assailant. It was an instinctive action born of necessity. Belatedly he realised he was giving his adversary every assistance. A knee jerked towards his groin. It rose too quickly, glancing off his hip. Then the whole leg coiled round his left leg like a boa constrictor.

His mind failed to find logical purpose. Pain throbbed through his right wrist. He did comprehend that his antagonist was using physical effort because he was unable to rely on other methods at present but the thought stopped short of offering helpful hints. The man held him secure till the twining leg succeeded. They fell over the corpse onto the floor. Every curl of breath sprang out of his lungs. His assailant crawled over him like a fair-sized gorilla. Strangler fingers seized his neck. He felt their ironlike pressure crush into his flesh and block his throat. He strained for air but it failed to get down his windpipe. The smell of sweat rose into his nostrils. His mind began to sway like a fairground swing.

He was on the verge of unconsciousness, scarlet light bubbling over his eyes, his hands unable to loosen those gripping his neck, listlessness creeping up his body, when the weight which held him down lost energy and the hands went slack. Then air was an anguish filing his throat. A face drooped lovingly on his. He lay still, too spent to shift the weight which nestled on him.

Her urgent whisper took on significance. 'You must try,' she kept saying.

Evidently she believed in miracles. Blood flapped over his eyes like blowing curtains. His throat ached atrociously.

She kept pleading: 'Try try try.' She sounded angry. Perhaps she thought he enjoyed lying on a corpse with a ton of sweaty something sprawled on him. He croaked at her. Gradually the weight rolled away.

He got to his knees. She stumbled at having to support him.

'How did you?' he got out and gave up while his throat throbbed like an exposed nerve for the second time in a few days. Slowly his hearing returned. Through a mush like static he heard her say: 'I took my gun from your pocket just now.' She sounded cool as if she had long experience of clobbering people. Perhaps she had taken correspondence lessons. Worse, an unmistakeable hint of amusement lightened her voice. She was entitled to it. The body on the floor with its face hidden so that you had to stoop to turn it over was a strip-cartoon trick and he had fallen for it.

Other normalities were returning. His lungs felt less like fairground balloons about to explode. His eyes were clearing. He saw her shoes illuminated by milky light from the torch lying about six feet away. His assailant kept groaning unmusically.

'Thanks,' he whispered sourly.

'You're welcome.'

He heard humour threading her whisper.

He got out: 'Well, what do you intend to do?'

'Oh, shoot you and drink your blood like vampires always do.'

He acted on the sarcasm that whipped through her whisper. His mind was too bothered to see an alternative if one existed. He went and retrieved the torch, flashing its light around till it picked out his automatic tucked alongside the dead man's ribs. She must have noted his hesitation for her voice told him impatiently to pick it up. Everything was quiet while he did so and flicked on the safety-catch.

He tried to act logically. There was opposition inside his skull. He felt a sense of victory at closing the door to the passage; it was without a lock. When he turned he saw that she had shut the door to the garden.

He went back to those on the floor, hauled the groaning man over onto his back and found one dream spot on his head and used the butt of the automatic to induce deeper sleep. That gave him a chance to go through the man's pockets. He transferred every likely discovery, mostly papers, to his own pockets for later examination. Finally he turned the light onto the unconscious face.

He and its owner were unacquainted. The face was Middle Eastern though European influences had subdued its strongest racial characteristics. It had a sort of appeal. There were women who would get woofy about it. You met such faces at places like Beirut, Alexandria, even Port Said, where Arabs and Europeans had commingled for centuries. The man was young and of impressive physique, twice the muscular development of most local men. The blue serge suit fitted him nicely. Its lapels were turned up to cover an open-necked white shirt.

'Chum of yours?'

'I've never seen him,' she whispered. 'What did he do with his shoes and socks?'

'Gave them to charity. Maybe he wanted you to admire his feet. Do that thing.'

He heard her breathe hard down her nose.

'How the hell can I tell?' he whispered. 'Ask a silly question.'

'Did he follow us round the house?'

'Did you see him leapfrog over it?'

Elliptically, she asked: 'Dorian, does your throat hurt?'

'I shall sing bass at La Scala tomorrow.'

'Should we get away? There may be others.'

He wished she would stop asking fool questions. 'There's still upstairs,' he reminded her. He got up and went back to the dead man and crouched down. Unhopefully, he took papers from one of the dead man's pockets and put them into an inside pocket. He searched down sleeve linings, the trouser turn-ups, inside the thighs. 'It might be better if you went back to the car,' he whispered. He stood up and flicked sweat off his forehead. 'If you decide to go, go,' he added. 'First, tell me a couple of things. Is either of them Sabri?'

She hesitated and then said: 'The dead man here is Ezad Iryani.'

'Oh,' he said blankly as if the name meant nothing to him and wondered if she was lying and why and how Iryani, the next man on the death list, came to be here. 'Ezad Iryani.'

'He comes from Dubai in the Persian Gulf. Do you know the man in the other room?'

'That's the second question I was going to ask you. He is familiar. I've seen him somewhere. Who is he?'

'I've never seen him till now.'

'Oh well. You must get to the car by starlight. I need the torch.'

'I worked alone till you came,' she whispered angrily.

'You needn't take pointless risks.'

'Dorian, I'm not leaving you alone.'

'Then don't blame me,' he whispered and his throat was anguish. 'Come on.'

They crept upstairs. Their caution was unrewarded. The rooms were empty. Unlike those below they were small, seven little rooms flanking one which probably rated as a master-bedroom and larger than three of them put together. None contained a stick of furniture. Their paintwork had greater variety than that downstairs. It implied what might be called a touch of sophistication. Each had its predominant tone: lilac, pink, heliotrope, peach, rose, ash grey, saffron, russet for the largest room. With slight forethought every tone of skin could appear better than nature had created it by placing it against a tone which enhanced or dramatised its other appeals. Particularly if you were eager. Particularly if the possessor of the tone under appraisal was a shade more responsive than a dead haddock. For instance, one of those African women slaves who were available in Saudi Arabia would look nice against the rose-coloured walls. But brothels usually supplied couches.

They went slowly downstairs. Her hand lay lightly on his arm. The stillness was so positive you felt you might bump into it. You could have heard a fly sneeze. As they got near the ground floor he imagined that outside the night held a distant throb. He halted and drew her alongside him. The throb did not come again. He went on, leading her up the hall. Her hand kept on his arm. She had lapsed back into her speechless mood. That helped. He had other need of his ears. It was often harder to get out than to get in.

At the worse possible time he was feeling tired. He longed to sprawl on a bed. Any bed provided it was givey. Just a great big cool gorgeous bed where he could stretch out his legs and twiddle his toes, bed without complications, an acre of bed where he could switch off body and mind and loll while the ruddy world went its own sweet way to perdition.

He switched off the torch.

He slid out through the door, automatic in hand, counted ten, drew her out, and stopped. Now, unmistakeably, there was a throb under the stars. It came from the north. Someone driving towards them was trying to toss every landspeed record onto the statistics dump. Light from far-off headlights dribbled over a section of darkness like melting ice-cream.

'Dorian?'

'They are coming a bit fast,' he agreed and glanced round, his eyes narrowed. Most of the garden seemed darker. He took her hand and tried to ignore his aching legs. They went down the three steps and along the path. He was unable to estimate how far off the car was at present. But he had to assume it had significance for them.

They went through the gateway.

This time he reacted faster. There were at least two of them. They flew out of the darkness on either side like bats. Formal introductions were skipped. As he told her to run a hand slashed meaningfully at his face. He swayed back on his heels. The knife missed his neck by several inches. Immediately it spun back, going past his eyes like a bacon-slicer. Then his arm reached over it. The barrel of his automatic jarred into the face of the knifer. If there was a yelp he did not hear it because of the raw cough of her automatic and the scream which followed it.

The opposition sought to speed things up. Another swing of the knife caught the front of his jacket, slashing through the fabric towards his right shoulder. The knifer played cautious, afraid to come too near. That was a mistake. As the knife went clear he kicked its owner in the belly. The knifer doubled up, sighing, tried to straighten and tried to get close. A crack on the head stopped him. He swayed like the last leaf in an autumn gale and fell on his face. His friend was already down there giving tongue in Arabic about rare anatomical freaks.

Once again the distant throb dominated the night. It was nearer. Too damn near.

'You?' he said curtly.

'Here,' she said, and he saw her crouched over the anatomical visionary searching his pockets.

He bent and arranged the head of the knifer and then clobbered him. At the second blow the knifer went out cold.

His unlovely face failed to awaken memory. His pockets contained a lot of paper currency from nearby sources but few documents. The real find was an old oilskin pouch.

'Are you ready?' she asked.

'Just a tick,' he said and opened the pouch. Its contents pleased him. He put it into another pocket.

As he went towards her the other man rose up off the ground and grabbed hold of her from behind. One dark-skinned hand closed over her face and yanked her head back. The other hand was plucking frantically at the belt holding his trousers.

Silk stepped past them and turned and cracked his gun down on the man's head. The man clung to her determinedly so he cracked him again and then swiped the barrel of the gun along the man's jaw. As the man let go of her he caught him, spun him round and kicked him in the groin. He had a descending sight of a lean, dark-skinned face with a large hooked nose and the heavy sensuous sort of lips you found among young homosexual Yemenis and Saudi Arabians. Then it was on the ground. Its owner writhed in agony.

He stooped over the man and pulled him onto his back. The tangle of long black hair came in handy even if it would have had every Beatle fan screaming envy. He sprawled on the ground like a drunken shepherd boy. Her shot had only ripped his arm.

'That car will be here soon,' she said sharply.

'I hear it.'

His hasty search produced a mess of folded greasy papers and another pouch, leather, larger than the first one. He stood up and shoved his legs into activity. These bouts of strong-arm stuff annoyed him. He was prickling all over from tension, his skin manufacturing so much sweat that he could have floated a paper boat in his navel if he had a paper boat.

They found the car unoccupied. He spent anxious seconds ascertaining if someone had decorated the engine with a blow-it-yourself bomb. Reassured, he shoved her inside and settled down behind the wheel, still prickling and annoyed. He switched on and put the car in gear. They began to move, driving without lights.

Less than a mile up the road he pulled off the verge as the distant headlight wands brightened perceptibly. His nerves fidgeted. He stopped and switched off. Those beams were like searchlights. The straight road was helpful. The lights swept along it like arrows and went past without slackening. At once he switched on the engine and drove back onto the road. He put up the lights.

'This may be rackety,' he warned, coughed drily, and increased speed up the road towards Amman.

Half an hour later recurrent claws of pain down his right arm forced him to slow down. He picked up the torch and turned its glow onto his chest. She gave an exclamation of alarm. His jacket and shirt had been sliced wide open. Blood from a cut had formed a ridge like dry sealing-wax which stuck his shirt to his chest. There was a slow ooze from a deeper cut across his biceps. His sleeve gaped down to the elbow.

'Stop the car and let me see,' she said.

'I'll live, little mother.'

'Must you be hostile now?'

'Did we start the evening as just good friends?' he asked and drew up. 'We're running short of juice.'

'There are cans in the boot.'

'I know,' he said. He shut off the engine and pocketed the keys. 'I'll fill her.'

'There's a first-aid kit in the back.'

'I know that too. Sit here and behave yourself.'

'Let me do it.'

'I can manage, woman,' he snarled.

It did not take long to empty two cans of petrol into the tank. He put them back into the boot, closed it, shook his head vigorously without ominous after-effects, and got the first-aid kit from the floor at the back. Around them the night snoozed like a well-fed baby, devoid of even the slightest sound from any quarter. He got back into the driving-seat and put the first-aid box on the seat between them.

'Let me drive,' she said.

'You may have to later,' he said. He turned to her and held out his hand. 'The gun.'

'I——'

'The gun.'

She gave it to him. 'Good girl,' he said, freed the clip of bullets and counted them, jerked it back and secured it, and put it into his left-hand pocket again. 'You have a little sleep.'

He drove faster after that. They ripped through Al Qatranah and As Suwaqah. Later they went through a night-darkened huddle which must have been Da'bah and raced up the road to Al Jizah. Soon after they passed it he swung off abruptly left round a fork into foothills.

'Where are we going?' she asked curtly.

'I need a bit of rest,' he answered practically. 'This road goes south to Ma'daba and Dhiban. If they're after us, they won't come down here. It'll give me a chance to clean myself up while you and I have a little chat.'

14

SHE leant her head back against the seat. He saw she was trembling as if from tension or fatigue or a combination of both, her hands shaking on her lap. At the touch of his hand on her shoulder she flinched, tensing as if to shrug it off, but lacked the willpower to abandon minor human contacts. Her lips stretched a little tighter.

'I'm all right,' she muttered drily. 'Just leave me alone. I am very resilient. What do you want to know?'

He took his hand off her shoulder.

'Several things. They can wait till you feel better.'

Her lips twisted acidly. 'You don't understand,' she said. 'You are cynical and callous. Childish too, though you have courage. You think what happened at that house was some sort of cops and robbers. You would. It means far more. But your outlook on life is too selfish and restricted to appreciate such things except excitement for kicks.'

He gave a soft whistle. 'And less than an hour ago we were Christian-naming each other,' he said wonderingly. 'It gets more like inter-party politics. At least, you were Christian-naming me, Miss . . . ?'

She disregarded the question put by his tone. After a pause she said: 'That man Ezad Iryani came behind Sabri on a death list.' Her eyes shifted restlessly under their lashes.

'Good gracious, is that all?' he queried. 'My poor child, there have been death lists hereabouts for the past four thousand years. You mustn't let such things get you. They're common as flies.'

'Oh, you fool!' she exclaimed. 'Few of them have been like this one.'

He interrupted. 'You are about to give me information,' he said. 'That's up to you. But if it's a pack of lies, don't waste your breath.'

His patent disbelief had the side-effect of calming her quicker than expressions of tender sympathy. She clenched her hands.

'If the people who prepared the list succeed in their plans there will be a *ji'haad*, a holy war,' she said and her deep voice was taut. 'Every country here will be involved. Millions of people will be killed. It may be the start of Armageddon. It will be if the Russians and Chinese conclude a temporary *rapprochement* like Hitlerite Germany had with Stalinist Russia. Khrushchov and Mao Tse-tung will not last forever. Their successors may conclude a deal on their immediate spheres of interest and postpone their ultimate clash. If they do, the Middle East will be dry grass waiting for the spark. How can anyone relax under such conditions?'

As she spoke her clenched hands began aimless gestures which were never completed. Her eyes flickered restlessly, searching the roof of the car. He knew how she felt. The spurt of energy which helped her when the effects of the drug wore off had gone and left her feeling drained. It had affected him similarly during his experimental test of the drug years ago.

He sighed. 'There are always plots here,' he scoffed.

'None like this,' she insisted.

'Most of them like this,' he said. 'People here are obsessed by legends of Armageddon getting off to a flying start in their home town. Sure, it may happen. Think of all the other places where it may happen. The notion presses hard here because this corner is a cradle of religions which have fought each other ceaselessly in order to survive. But I've news for you. Right now we can't do much about it, can we? So stop whipping yourself.'

'You are ignorant about these people.'

'Everybody is ignorant about everybody. This is the age of newspapers full of stories about the loneliness of the individual. This is the age of weeping over togetherness. Ham.'

'That has nothing to do with the situation here.'

'The chances are nothing will happen here,' he said. 'Why? Because the basic interests of Arabs and Israelis in this age are identical. What keeps them apart are religions, fanatics, and propaganda. It's unreal, it's futile, it's old hat, it's primitive, and it's just plain childish. Sooner or later Israel and the Arabs must make their peace and work together. It's an economic necessity. You'll learn.' He yawned. 'Now, what shall we do? Tell each other funny stories or play pat-a-cake?'

She kept still. Her face was tense and tired. Muscles at the angle of her jaw kept jerking. Only temporary weakness plus a measure of trust acquired from these hours kept her quiet. If she had felt stronger she would have got out to start walking home.

He changed his method. She was passive as he freed her slightly so he could get his hand behind her neck to knead the muscles. Gradually her lips lost their stiffness. He went on massaging her neck and said: 'You mean an Arab attack on Israel. So perhaps you're a Sabra.'

Her eyes turned towards him. She remained quiet, unsatisfied by his conversational tone. 'Sabra' was the Arabic word for cactus fruit, reputedly sweet inside its tough and prickly skin. It was also the name given to native-born Israelis. The faintest sigh died in her throat. She moistened her lips.

'You're mean,' she said. 'You sprung that on me. What makes you think I'm an Israeli?'

Her voice was defiant.

He raised his brows fractionally. 'We had a conversation on our drive to that house,' he reminded her. 'Maybe I'm wrong. The American accent creeps through when you get forgetful. But Americans have a different view of events here from yours. Anyway, it's your business. But you did pull me into it. I'm entitled to be curious.'

'I told you why I wanted your help.'

'You told me a lot of lies. Would you like a drink of your brandy?'

'Are you trying to get me drunk?'

'Oh, my God! Very well, I'll bear the idea in mind.'

She freed her head from his hand. 'You were going to ask me questions,' she said.

'I said we would have a chat.'

'It's the same thing.'

'If you like,' he said. 'You'd better give me some details straight. I've had enough excitement. And you've got an unfair advantage. You've been asleep.'

'Poor boy,' she said unsympathetically. 'Why are men so damn frail?' She stretched without stark enthusiasm for physical effort.

'It's the way our Mums made us.'

She said nothing for several moments, then she nodded. 'I'll have a drink,' she said.

He reached over the seat and picked up the flask. At her invitation he unscrewed the top, took out the stopper, and poured brandy into the top. She took it from him and tasted it carefully. Her eyes watched his face steadily. The tip of her tongue licked the corners of her lips. Then she swallowed the remaining brandy at a gulp and coughed drily. As they watched each other she turned the small top upside down to show it was empty. A bead of liquor fell off the rim onto the floor. She held the top out to him.

'Now you,' she said.

He drank it willingly, feeling the raw spirit warm his belly and lessen some of the cold in him from events of the past few hours. She took another drink which he poured out for her.

'Where do you want to begin?' she asked.

'At the beginning. You. Reporters have greater confidence if they can trust people who say they have a story.'

'Will you believe me?'

'Try me.'

She swallowed the brandy without one blink and handed the top back to him.

Around them the night was a canopy of silence. She told her story. It seemed that she was an American. She and her parents lived in New York. Her brothers, two in number, and younger sister, had married, and gone to other parts of the States. At this point complications entered the story. Her maternal grandmother was Jewish and had emigrated to America with her parents while a child. Her father's father was an Egyptian orphan who had also gone to New York from London. These elders were still very much alive, hardy and resolute, thoroughly enjoying their beloved vendetta. It appeared that among the children of her family she was the only one who had a flair for languages.

'Uh-huh,' he said. 'I'm with you.'

She smiled wrily. 'It was pretty bad,' she said, and told him how her parents managed to keep the peace by letting her be taught Arabic, Hebrew, and Yiddish. Directly she left college she began work for a United Nations agency. She told him honest-seeming episodes of how her grandparents continued to fight each other through her till she was sent to Egypt two years ago where, from the outset, Egyptians she met had taken her for Jewish in the belief that any woman who came from America was devoid of even one drop of Arab blood. During a quarrel over another matter one woman had accused her of being an American Jewess spying for Israel. She shrugged.

'So some of them ganged up on you,' he commented.

'People who've gotten an urge can be real spiteful,' she said evenly. 'I guess they enjoyed feeling themselves loyal Egyptians defending their security against an enemy in their midst. As of then I felt like an Israeli. I gave up my job. Here I am . . . you haven't asked my name.'

He glanced out at the darkness. 'We'll get to it later,' he

said casually. 'That isn't the whole story, is it? You were very fond of your grandmother.'

She hesitated. 'She has had her problems,' she said bleakly.

'Okay, I'll take that story.'

'Don't you think it strange or unusual?'

'It may be to you. I've heard stranger stories. You've lived it. Now, tell me about this supposed American, Dominis. I imagine he is Russian.'

When she kept silent he glanced at her and saw warmth in her eyes. 'I underestimated you,' she said contritely. 'You act too lazy to think, just a man who enjoys danger. Yes, his name is Muhammed Shvernik. His mother came from Azerbaijan. His father is a Muscovite. He's another racial mixture like me. Pure-bred Englishmen don't understand what it's like to be a minor United Nations.'

'Leave your claws in storage. Why is he here?'

'He's trying to find the Prophet.'

'Well, bless his heart and the best of Kremlin luck to him.'

'I don't mean the Muslim Mahomet.'

'Oh, I know which Prophet you mean.'

Her eyes widened. 'You've heard about him?' she asked.

'His nom-de-plume has got around. Rumours, you know. Lazy though I am, my ears flex themselves. Is he mixed up in this?'

'He is this,' she said positively.

Little of what she told him was new. Most of it was similar to what he had read on the slip which got into his pocket. There were other names. What was original concerned nameless friends of hers who located Sabri and Iryani, who had been prepared to expose the whole story about the Prophet in exchange for money and safety in Israel to start a new life somewhere else with capital.

'Another drink?' he suggested as she paused.

She nodded. 'If you'll keep pace with me,' she said.

He poured it out and gave it to her. 'Now,' he prompted.

She took a sip of the brandy and then held the metal cap carefully in the fingers of both hands. Sabri and Iryani had been lodged in the house of a friend of hers at Amman. They were going to be taken to Jerusalem and then across the frontier. While there they had gone out, both of them disguised, and had seen one of the Jordan group, the local cell for the Prophet, whoever he might be. That night Sabri had disappeared. Her friend learned that he fled to Jerusalem in a bid to get over the frontier by himself; the story had come from Iryani who also told her friend that Sabri had stayed at the Isis. Her friend told her to try to find Sabri. That night Iryani also vanished from the Amman hideout. She had gone to the Isis and heard that Sabri was staying there under his own name.

'Can you believe such a fool thing?' she demanded.

'I think so,' he said. 'He stayed there before. He may have felt secure by being himself instead of hiding. Frightened men do queer things. Why were you down at the Dung Gate?'

'He got in touch with my friend and told them he was in Jerusalem and would go through with it if I met him and got him across into Israel, but he needed money first.'

'That suggests somebody had recognised him and was blackmailing him fast. So you took it. How much?'

'About five hundred pounds.'

'Had you met him?'

She shook her head. 'No,' she said and had another drink.

He thought for a bit and then nodded. 'You went there, he did not turn up, you kept watch on the Isis and finally decided to get into his room,' he said.

'Yes,' she agreed. 'Tell me why you went to the Gate.'

'I had a tip-off that a man named Sabri wanted to sell a big story and arranged to meet him there,' he said. 'But someone, presumably whoever was blackmailing him, had him under close watch. They must have followed him. On each of the two evenings I went there people tried to knife me. Here I am . . . with another knifer back at that house. Queer coincidence. Go on.'

'Soon after you left the room that Chinese came,' she said. 'I think he thought I was Sabri's mistress. He did not stay as long as you did.'

'Bad taste,' he said gallantly. 'Then what?'

She had left the hotel and got her car and stayed outside the hotel all night. Soon after dawn she had seen a man whom she thought was Sabri arrive with two men in another car. They left again within minutes. She had followed them.

'To that house?'

'Yes.'

'Why did you imagine it was Sabri?'

'I had a description of him.'

'Then you followed.'

'There was more traffic on the roads. When I got back to Jerusalem I could not contact my friend. I thought of you.'

As she finished her drink he glanced round at the darkness. Warm air coming through the open window coiled over his face. 'Well,' he said at length, 'it brings up other questions, doesn't it? You'll have to give me other details. So far is just not far enough.'

Her hand reached out and her fingers slid between his. 'I can't tell you everything,' she said unsurely.

'No,' he agreed. 'Let me theorise. Sabri and Iryani are important to the Prophet because they were key men in his organisation. So both of them were taken to that house, which means it must be a Prophet house. My guess is it was intended to be a place where prospective members of the Prophet organisation who have a weakness for women could be accommodated. They were held there until by some means they staged a fight. Iryani got killed but Sabri got clear. And where is our wandering boy now? Echo answers where?'

'I don't know.'

'How about the other men, particularly the second corpse? It sounds quite Shakespearian, doesn't it?'

'He and they were strangers to me.'

'Sure?'

'I'm sure,' she said querulously.

He played abstractedly with her lax fingers. They were warmer now, long and strong. He heard the bicycle-pump squeak of bats wheeling overhead. 'Well, they're pretty flamboyant,' he said. 'The whole set-up is pretty ancient though it serves modern ends. There are things I don't understand about your friend Sabri. His defection from the Prophet's organisation may have been a dodge to uncover a suspected traitor who was believed to be in touch with your friend—them, as you call whoever your friend is or are. You'd better find out if Iryani was first to get in touch and offer the story. If Iryani was first, then we may discover Sabri was sent out to get him. That would explain why Sabri is doing an *Edward, My Son*—you remember the play built around a character who never appeared? Sabri sits awkwardly in my mind.' He freed her hand. 'My turn for the brandy. Did you ever meet Sabri?'

'No,' she said.

'Stay strangers,' he advised and poured himself a drink. He drank it thoughtfully. 'This isn't bad. Not French.'

She smiled. 'Spanish,' she said.

'Ah, very good. I remember sitting outside one of those Madrid restaurants near the station drinking brandy at tenpence a glass with a retired British Army officer who had become a tourist guide and was an expert on the Duke of Wellington's campaign in the Peninsular War. Very good. What with that and the Prado just up the road full of those gorgeous pictures by Goya and the Flemish painters . . . boy! Do you like pictures painted by artists?' he asked and finished his drink and poured her another.

After some moments she said: 'I'm getting odd ideas. Dorian, I would like to talk to you about politics and death and love and why we are here.'

'Let's fix to do that some weekend. We can take our sandwiches somewhere quiet, like the moon—no, not that corner, somewhere really free from people and machinery. How's the brandy?'

She said mmmm lazily and stretched her back. 'Better now,' she said.

'Right, now this,' he said and got out the treasure-trove stuffed into his pockets.

The description put its value a shade high. At first glance it appeared to be the usual personal clutter though the letters might yield worthwhile information during proper examination. Three items rewarded his present shuffle. On a dirty and creased sheet of paper taken from the man who attacked him was a list of names which began with those on the original slip put into his pocket and went on to include others. He was pretty sure most of the additional names were the sort you found among those handkerchief-sized states along the Persian Gulf. He told her his opinion. The other two were the small pouches. Each contained a long steel needle, narrow strips of bamboo, a circular metal disc similar to a hollowed-out thermos flask stopper, and a plastic phial like a liquid detergent container but less than one-third standard size. She sat wordless while he upended one phial above a disc and squeezed gently. A drop of dark substance like honey oozed into the disc. He stared at it thoughtfully.

Her hand came on his arm. 'I asked what it is,' he heard her say.

'One of the original dream-it-yourself aids. The great-grandpa of Aldous Huxley's "soma" and other tranquillisers. To be precise, the sap extracted from pods of *papaver somniferum*. In a word, opium.'

'Opium!'

For some moments he went on looking at it. 'Yes,' he said finally. He rolled the equipment back into the pouches and put them into his pockets. 'Yes, opium,' he said again and wiped a hand over his face. The skin was so dry and tired it damn nearly rustled. 'Fascinating, isn't it?'

They sat quiet side by side busy with their separate thoughts. Once another squeak of bats wheeled overhead. His mind enjoyed a little holiday without one tiptoe towards sleep. He felt her put the flask cap into his hand. Then she realised that was an error so she took it back and drank the brandy herself and gave him the empty cap.

Minutes later she stretched her arms. Her long fingers spread wide and she gave a shiver of tiredness. She folded her hands together on her lap. 'How do we share?' she asked. 'Do you have the ground while I have the car or do you prefer the car? You decide.'

He shrugged but said nothing.

'You won't believe me if I say I will act sensibly by your opinion of what is sense,' she said gravely. 'But you have a real safeguard. Somewhere inside that complex mind of yours is information about the Prophet which I haven't got. You needn't deny it. I am sure of it. People do have intuition, you know. I'd be the biggest fool in the world to risk losing whatever you can tell me and my friend.'

He reached a decision unwillingly, reluctant to make an effort. 'I imagine we can share a car here without anyone saying you have compromised me,' he said and sat up yawning wearily. 'You can have the front seat. Just behave yourself. Neither of us will be really asleep and I have the artillery.'

'May I go for a walk?'

'Want to borrow a piastre?'

As she headed off into the darkness he took the opportunity to go for a stroll to admire the view in the opposite direction while he thought over what had happened. He was pretty sure now that the note had got into his pocket by accident. Somebody in Marraqesh had mistaken him for a contact or member of the Prophet organisation and once again that showed how damn clumsy they were. Clumsy but effective like heavyweight wrestlers.

When he got back to the car, circling his injured arm

slowly, she sat on the ground beside the car. Her head was lowered, her hair like a scatter of blown leaves, her legs drawn under her. She was drawing circles in the loose soil. He sat down beside her still flexing his arm.

'It's hot inside the car,' she said.

'We'll have to be brave about it.'

'How are those cuts?'

'This time I may just live but cherish me.'

She held out her hand, palm upward. 'You didn't find this one,' she said. 'It was underneath the chassis.'

It was another ignition key. He took it and put it into a pocket, looking at her. He saw her neat lips give him their tiny cool smile.

15

NOFRET GOHAR leant slightly back, only slightly, from the waist, her hands keeping tight hold on his arms.

Afternoon sunlight coming through the shuttered windows of the house at Hamadan Road zebra-striped the wall which flanked the harpsichord. It showed her long eyes were wholly free from grief. Within moments of his being admitted by a slender half-African girl with huge eyes and broad sulky lips she had hastened in to welcome him tempestuously. Even at contact the calorific level of her greeting was several significant degrees higher than their leavetaking yesterday, a candid statement that she had filled the interval with thoughts more scorching than mere nostalgia. Since then he had found the afternoon heat increase.

Her sleeveless wrapover white cotton frock had every sign of being one of those simple little things women fling on in the right emergency. A broad white belt partly secured it round her waist but the top buttons were undone, revealing an expanse of rich skin. Whatever she wore under the frock was no obstacle. An obsessive musky scent came from her immaculately tidy hair. Nothing about her manner suggested the sorrowful widow. He felt vaguely intimidated, unfamiliar with women who raced at him as if he was the last representative of the vital weaker sex left alive. He was pleased to see that her bruises were better and wished her fingers would lessen their grip on places where his own stung most often.

Her moist-lipped smile seemed wholly spontaneous. 'I

have never felt so lonely in my life,' she said yet again. 'I had almost decided to be completely reckless and come to you.' Her caressing voice lent every syllable the quality of an endearment.

He smiled. 'Haven't they come back yet?' he asked.

She shook her head. 'No,' she answered pleasedly. 'Allah be praised for His mercy, they have been delayed. I am so glad.'

He let his gaze roam over her raised face and shapely shoulders. Even men devoid of imagination would have a pretty shrewd idea of how she must appear when her only covering was her hair. The shape of her nude arms was so perfect that they could have been put on the Venus di Milo without causing an international flurry. They would awaken the impersonal lust of every collector, impel him to go on uncovering her to find one visible blemish. She might have divined his thoughts for her smile widened.

'I thought they might be here,' he said aimlessly.

She feigned annoyance. 'Must we talk about them?' she asked.

'They give me an excuse to mix pleasure with business,' he reminded her and smoothed his hand slowly up her curved back.

She trembled. 'Only pleasure?' she questioned.

'I'm a simple Englishman. I need time to create ecstasy.'

'You must create chances . . . you look tired.'

'I was awake most of the night. Thinking.'

'Ah,' she breathed. 'You too . . . *sahlim ideeq*, blessed be thy hands.' She put her arms round him and closed her eyes. 'Kiss me.'

He created the chance to browse on her neck and smell her perfume. They were pleasant occupations. Her lips parted directly his reached them. She sighed and fitted herself nearer and her tongue sought his. She was no flimsy doll yet her body was seemingly weak against his. Her strong hands slid down to his hips and held him possessively. No well-mannered man could refuse such hospitality. He believed in good manners.

When he came up for air her face had a rapt expression. She kept her eyes shut, her lips open. He saw that her hair was likely to topple down her back. A sigh came from her throat. She reverted to poetic provocation.

'Man, must I die of thirst for the wine of thy love to revive me?' she murmured huskily. 'Must thou torment me? O man, since we parted my body has been a desert burnt by merciless heat awaiting thy presence to give it freshness and meaning. Thou hast obsessed my senses. Thy vigour and strength torment me. I think of thee through every minute. I crave to be the instrument under thy hands. Must thou deny us the solace of our passion? I await thee. Must time mock our failure to fill these hours? Thy need is my delight. O lion, thou would find me thy true mate.'

'Woman, time is the enemy of lovers,' he reminded her bleakly. 'It opposes even those who live to rejoin each other. Life forces patience on us though ultimately it goes unrewarded for many. Is it not true that thy sweetness is for me a forbidden pool?'

She gave no sign of response to his mention of death. Her face was taut for another reason, her eyes lidded for another purpose. Her hands went over him ceaselessly, gathering memory with some candour. 'O beloved, it is eager to refresh thee and regain its purpose in the truth thou can give it by thy need,' she whispered.

'I shall return.'

She kept her face raised and would have fallen if he let go of her. He moved his lips on the side of hers and felt her shudder. Her hands came up to lift his head. She opened her eyes unwillingly. Their trancelike gaze did not really focus on him. She was breathing rapidly.

'You came to tell me you are going away,' she said in pedestrian English, her voice flat.

'I must work.'

'Damn your work!' she said violently. 'It's taking you from me—now. Now! How can I——'

'Quietly. Demanding women frighten me.'

After a moment anger died away from her face and her stiff lips regained their crumpled softness though her brows frowned. She continued to lean back against his arm and her hands clenched fiercely on his shoulders.

'You are right, *ya aziz*, O beloved. I shall not frighten you away from me. Will you come back?'

'*Insh'allah.*'

'When?' she demanded petulantly.

'Well, you know how it is for newspapermen. We get blown about by wars and revolutions and assassinations and rumours. Particularly by rumours. If my programme goes according to order I'll be here again pretty soon.'

'When?' she reiterated impatiently.

'Roughly three months,' he lied. 'Maybe sooner. It depends on things outside my control.'

She grimaced. One coil of hair had finally begun to tumble down her back like shining black water. He gathered an impression that she enjoyed how his free hand fondled her. She kept moving quietly against him. Her eyes were alert now.

'Will we meet?' she asked nervously.

'That was one reason why I came.'

'It's all right about him. He can't expect anything from me. Too much has gone wrong between us. I am meaningless for him.'

'Muslims have rigorous beliefs about the faithfulness of women.'

She smiled sardonically. 'A man must be a man if his woman is to show him traditional obedience,' she said. 'In this age women are no longer involuntarily muslim, resigning ones, unless they are peasants. We are fighting for our rights. He is nothing, only Amer's thing. He is jelly,' she said contemptuously.

'There is something else.'

'What else can keep us apart?'

'My job keeps me shifting around.'

'You mean I want a man who seldom leaves me,' she

said and trembled. Abruptly she switched the line of conversation. 'Why have you come here, brought me joy, given me hope, let me hold you and speak of my love, if we have to part without a dream of tomorrow in my heart?'

'First, reverting to chances, I thought you might be here.'

The answer left her unsatisfied. 'What else?' she asked sullenly.

'Do you remember Amer told me he would let me have a list and samples? They haven't arrived at my hotel. He said they were at his warehouse. How do I get there?'

As she watched his eyes her fingers kept up their continual pressure on his muscles.

'Have you a car?' she asked and her unsteady voice implied a struggle between concentration on what they were saying and their physical nearness. Her lips were unsteady.

'No.'

'It is some distance from here, several miles. They have left a key here.'

'Oh well, I've got feet.'

Her head gave a tiny shake. 'The warehouse staff is away,' she said. 'But one of our cars is in the garage. We can take it. You can drive while I show you the route. Then you can bring me back.'

'Can you spare the time?'

She answered obliquely through another question. 'Do you want to see me again?' she asked huskily.

'I don't see myself getting a fortune from dolls,' he countered, and supposed he should feel sorry for her because she had a tragic weakness, sorry too on account of her dead husband, but they were not exactly at the explanations or hairshirt stage.

He saw the glazed look spread over her long eyes again. '*Ya aziz*, I will tell thee what I want,' she muttered thickly and did so in Arabic until she was past words, her mouth clinging to his, and she gave a moan of excitement, drawing his breath into her throat. With a sinuous writhe the thin dress was off her shoulders and under his hands was naked skin, sleek skin, and rich, pliant flesh. She twisted lightly against him.

He felt a bit beset. It was natural. Upon occasion his impulses were one thousand per cent. average primitive, Adam's grandpa licking prurient lips over possibilities. This was such an occasion. He had damn good cause. In this mood she was not the sort of woman you wanted to brush off even though you guessed her weakness. This reality was gorgeous.

She was superbly rash, a fully-grown headstrong woman full of murmurous incitements to folly. You could shuffle through fifty lives without getting near loudhailer distance of any woman like her in this mood. And behind her now were generations of women going through life fighting to preserve their position by the sheer recklessness and fury of their passion, fighting other wives, concubines too, rather than have their man say 'I divorce thee' thrice and send them back to their families.

'Must we go?' her mouth pleaded against his on a broken breath. 'We are alone here. They will not disturb us.'

He was sorely tempted. When you heard such a woman moan in your arms other considerations weighed as heavy as thistledown. She knew it and took delight in this chance to disclose her innate skills. Her mouth and knowledgeable whispers incited him.

He tried to yank his attention towards reality. His good intention was a non-starter. With her mouth murmurous against his, the provocative brush of her body on his tantalising him, he felt pretty good. He hadn't felt like this for a long time. She was catching fire from her own incitements. Her body was trembling and weak in his hold. Words blurred into a moan in her throat. His self-control slid. This was lovely hell. He saw right the way through it but it was still lovely hell. Fifteen months was a long old while for every man except eunuchs and the incredible Swann.

Swann.

Infernal man.

He got hold of her hands and eased her slightly away. She was shaking. Her forehead fell onto his shoulder, the unhappy one naturally. Breath soughed from her mouth. Her hands gripped his shoulders to keep herself erect. He shifted his hands to her waist.

'We must go,' he said.

'No . . .'

'I will come back.'

'It won't be now,' her muffled voice said pleadingly.

'Don't I know it . . . but then we won't have to rush.'

'Are you sure? Sure?'

'Haven't you given me cause to come back?'

After some moments she lifted her head and looked at him. 'I expect you are right,' she said reluctantly and lowered her arms. She was breathing unsteadily. 'But you may regret it.'

'Won't we enjoy ourselves if we are not hurried?'

She smiled ruefully and drew the dress up over her shoulders. A cascade of shining hair fell between her breasts. She drew a deep breath. 'I'll put on another dress,' she said bleakly and glanced sideways at him from those long eyes. Then she turned and left the room.

He wiped his forehead. It had been near as a toucher. He could feel the sinuous sway of her body against him. Beyond question it would be a memorable experience. He overcame various impulses to follow her. Instead he counted ten and heeled round.

Deeper in the house the half-African girl was singing gently to herself. Her voice had a rich liquid lilt. Along a nearby road a car purred through the heavy sunshine. There was a soft tring like passing birdsong. Those were the positive sounds. Inside him was a private zizz.

He went to the open windows and stepped out into the loveless garden. Seen in daylight it was even more forlorn than at night. While he drew air deep into his lungs he glanced round. After a pause he turned, took one of the small tie-clip bugs from a pocket, made it live, and went over to the wall of dolls. He fixed it out of sight among the tinsel golden robes of a cute angel doll. As he finished the task he hummed an aimless tune which let him mumble an equally aimless lyric that contained the words 'follow the car' while he activated another bug in the small cigarette-pack and stowed it inside his breast-pocket.

Out of sight the girl sang fluently. He was sure it must be the half-African girl; only a throat which owed much to Africa could have such natural liquid richness of timbre. She was singing a lullaby. He went to the harpsichord and pulled out the stool and sat down. After vamping chords he played pieces guaranteed to calm rather than induce mass hysteria or grim shuffle.

When Nofret Gohar came into the room he saw she had changed her mind. A quirk of female guile had prompted her to keep on the white dress though it was so neat now over her magnificent bosom that it would have appeared darn near demure if he was without memory of how she looked when it was a dishevelled nuisance.

As she walked lazily across the room he stood up. The broad shiny black belt drew attention to her immaculate hair. She wore fashionable black shoes. On her left arm hung a black handbag large enough to contain a fair-sized automatic. Both white and black enhanced the dusky warmth of her skin. The fingers of her right hand held the gilt bullet which Swann regarded as deadlier than anything inside a gun. Her face wore an in-public expression but as they looked at each other it changed to the most candid expression of sexual desire he had ever seen. She licked her naked lips, her gaze meeting his steadily.

'You see what you do to me?' she said.

'You know what you do to me and every man.'

Her lips flinched. 'Don't talk about them,' she said sharply.

'You must know how you affect them.'

'I don't want to think of another man.'

'Then you needn't.'

She smiled and raised her face. 'Before I smear this stuff on,' she ordered.

He took full advantage of what might be his last chance.

As she drew away she seemed to be on the verge of saying something. Instead she smiled tautly and her shoulders gave a shivery motion. She opened her bag and took out a mirror and drew the cap off the lipstick. Her brows frowned slightly while she smoothed the stick along her lips and then moved them over each other. She put the cap back on the gilt bullet and glanced at him from her long eyes.

'The right colour?'

'Too fashionable,' he said. 'I prefer the bare truth.'

'Have I used too much?'

'Why risk catching cold?'

'I would sooner stay here if both of us risked catching pneumonia.'

'You're learning my patois.'

'It's infectious,' she said and sighed. 'We must go or I shall change our minds.'

She walked impatiently ahead of him out of the french windows, her long legs hastening them to the garage. He opened its wide double doors and was greeted by strong petrol fumes and a newish pearl-grey Consul with turquoise blue upholstery whose bonnet was almost cool under his fingers. The adjacent stable-space was empty. Alongside the walls was the usual litter of tools and tins. Both front doors of the Consul were unlocked and he saw the ignition-key in its socket. As he settled behind the wheel he saw that she evidently found it strange to occupy the front seat and sat tensely erect. He switched on the engine and put the car in gear and backed out. The drive was wide enough for reversing without difficulty.

Near the gateway he asked: 'Which way?'

'South. It's on the road to Bayt Lahm, Bethlehem.'

'Which road? Through Abu Dis?'

'Past the UN headquarters,' she said curtly.

He turned down Jericho Road. The traffic was the usual hodge-podge of Arab and Western patterns, horsemen of Old Testament mien who jogged past habited Christian monks striding on sandals, tottery elders exchanging current *faddhl* in thin shade cast by cypresses, turbaned *mullahs*, tourist cars, military trucks. Near the UN Truce Supervision HQ a meek traffic jam of *jahaishi*, little donkeys, milled about like fairground roundabouts. He kept glancing at the driving mirror but it was empty of the car which should be following.

'Relax,' he said. 'People will think we've had an up-and-downer like married folk.'

'I would love to quarrel with you. There would be afterwards.'

Thereafter they scarcely spoke. Their few exchanges were on the same level. She ignored his invitation to relax. Although he paid little attention to her he was conscious of her physical tension. Occasionally he glanced at the mirror. He could have spared himself the effort. The plan had gone wrong. There was no sign of the other car.

Near the bulge of the Israeli frontier they met a Bedu family, proud as Lucifer despite their rags, their *lithams*, turbans, wound close about their heads. Farther on they passed a group of idle fawnlike youths, their pouting-lipped faces disdainful. Then came two lorries full of singing nuns. He took another look at the mirror. It was empty of his hopes. He wiped a finger knuckle over his lips. He was on his own. For some reason his cuts started to prickle.

He got out his handkerchief and wiped his neck. 'Which side is it?' he asked.

She misunderstood his question. 'This side round the left-hand fork,' she replied absently. 'Lend me your handkerchief.'

'It's a bit dish-clothy.'

'Should I care?' she asked and took it and wiped her wrists and the palms of her hands. Then she held it as if she wanted to tear it to shreds.

Within moments her voice claimed his attention. They had just passed a clump of trees. 'There it is,' she said and pointed at a square and utilitarian, dun-coloured building like a large flat-roofed barn three hundred yards from the first of a row of poverty-smitten cottages. It stood back about twenty yards from the road. He saw a telephone cable leading to a point on the right-hand wall. In front of it an oblong noticeboard on concrete posts proclaimed the Arabic equivalent of 'Holy Land Eternal Radiance Souvenirs Ltd'.

He drew up alongside the noticeboard where the car was clearly visible to other travellers, switched off the engine and sat looking at the building without attempting to get out. Its narrow brown-painted door was shut. Two visible windows were shuttered. There was no sign of human activity. Down the road two *fijirias*, virgins of marriageable age, sunned their childish faces while they stared wistfully at passing cars and dreamed their dreams. Boys rode by on twitchy-eared donkeys. Farther on a shaven-headed small boy did his very best to help an old boulder to grow.

Suddenly she said: 'Stay here while I get them.'

'I'll come with you.'

'It will save time. I know where they are.'

'I'll come with you,' he repeated.

She slid her hand between his knees. 'It will only take me a moment,' she pleaded. 'Then we can go back and be together.'

'I'd be nervous with you in there while I litter up the sunshine.'

His mild tone evidently nonplussed her. While she was silent her hand squeezed his thigh as if to reassure herself that he had muscles. Through the lightweight fabric her fingers were warm and strong. He was pretty sure they could serve instinctively every subtle impulse of her volatile nature.

'Please wait here,' she begged. 'I won't be long.'

He turned his attention from the hopeful small boy to

her. She searched his eyes for a long moment. Then her lips lost their softness. Abruptly her hand was a clenched fist beating impotently on his leg. He laid it back on her lap and reclaimed his handkerchief. An expression of resignation came into her eyes. She looked away.

'We could have been happy together,' she said violently.

'Come on,' he said, and pocketed the ignition key and reached across to open the door for her. Then he opened the one on his side and got out into the late afternoon sunshine. He shut the door quietly. He looked round. There was no sight of the other car. He was very much on his own.

16

SHE was wordless on their walk to the warehouse door. Although her step matched his one glance at her profile showed him that her face was set and her lovely lips thrust forward in an expression uncalculated to entice, giving them the sort of sullen fury you saw on the faces of women drivers trying to cope with big city traffic miseries. Near the door she opened her bag and extracted a key whose size qualified it for service during the ceremony of keys at the Tower of London. It took an effort on her part to turn it in the lock. The door opened, screeching like a tortured owl. She would have left the key there but he took it out and dropped it into his pocket. They went forward into a darkness which was notable for its absence of thick heat and dust.

'Wait,' she said worriedly. 'The light switch is over—ah.'

He blinked at the sudden glare of yellow light which flooded the warehouse. To all intents they had it to themselves. There was an absence of dust except on the floor. He sniffed at the air. It was comparatively fresh, lacking the close heat of places here which had been closed for even one day.

In front of them were long trestle tables heaped with thousands of dolls wearing rainbow-coloured silk attire. Some heaps were instantly recognisable from a distance; hundreds of the Virgin in her blue gown, hundreds of white and glittery gold angels, hundreds of woolly black-bearded Greek Orthodox priests like tiny replicas of that man in Cyprus, two rows of Mary Magdalens in flamboyant finery before the seven devils were cast out of her. Most of them had their separate tables. Along the walls were piles of brown cardboard and shiny white boxes.

She started forward. Instantly he caught hold of her shoulder. At the same moment he heeled the door shut. He swung her round to face him. Clearly she was an unhappy woman at present. Her eyes avoided his. She trembled as his hand went down her back to rest on her hip. She frowned perplexedly.

'Your bag,' he said.

'Why?' she asked nervously.

'Give it to me.'

Unwillingly she held it out. He opened it and searched it for a gun or a knife or a syringe. Then he tested the frame. He handed it back to her. She forced herself to look at him, her eyes full of conflicting emotions. He knew she was disliking this episode intensely. She moistened her lips.

'Please wait outside,' she said again, her voice unfamiliarly weak, pleading without hope.

He patted her arm. 'I've come this far,' he said. She drew her breath sharply as he got his automatic from his shoulder holster. 'Just a precaution,' he told her. 'We might be held up. The damnedest things happen nowadays. I must protect us.'

She did her best to convey tolerant amusement. Her eyes betrayed her. 'Are you always cautious?' she asked mockingly.

Their voices had an echoey hollowness in the big warehouse. It gave an eerie acoustical effect of bouncing each word back off the walls. Over on the right, behind her, was a tiny office compartment. Its small glass windows were empty of human shapes.

'Ever since the life insurance people refused me,' he said. 'I'm nervous, you know, my stomach full of pills. Shake me and I tinkle for hours.' He waved his gun at the office. 'Let's see if anyone is having a conference there.'

'You go,' she said stiffly.

'Ladies first,' he said ungallantly.

She wanted to defy him but lacked the resolution. Her eyes strove to hint that she was beginning to doubt his sanity. She did not succeed. Abruptly she wheeled and almost ran to the office compartment and opened its door.

He went into it one pace behind her. It was empty. It was without a ceiling. In the centre stood an oblong table heaped with dolls and boxes. Against one wall was the great-grandmother of rolltop desks, open, the writing space littered with letters, a black telephone alongside the dusty sepia photograph of four women veiled as heavily as Tuaregs. Against another wall was an oblong table, smaller, its top hidden by letters, and two ancient wooden filing cabinets. The two wooden chairs had an atmosphere of arthritic infirmity. He sniffed at the air without locating noticeable reminders of humanity or dust. He touched her shoulder.

'Right,' he said.

Instantly she wheeled out past him, then swung round to face him. Her eyes did their utmost to read his. She smiled half-heartedly.

'Why did you search my bag?'

He looked at her levelly. 'Well, you really do know, don't you?' he countered. 'It's obvious. You did what Amer told you to do. Perhaps he usually gave you instructions through your husband. Today he gave you orders direct.'

Something youthful went out of her face. Suddenly it was just the face of another woman, lovely because it had grown in beauty without assistance from herself. She tried to check the transformation by appearing incredulous. But the lines at the corners of her eyes and the tension of her lips told their own story. Lovely, oh yes, but youth had gone.

'What are you talking about?' she asked unsurely.

'Must we fool each other?' he asked gently. 'We understand each other pretty well in the basic relationship. What I'm saying is that I have got just sufficient wits to realise that Amer sent you to see me. You were told to find out if I had seen Sabri. It was clumsy. Amer is clumsy. Damn clumsy. Well, clumsiness is part of life. You should have stayed out of it. You're too gorgeous to go wasting.'

She did what she could to let her eyes imply incredulity. It was unsuccessful. She was a bad actress, able to dissemble only in one role. 'Has this anything to do with me?' she got out blankly.

'Yes, you've let it have something to do with you, haven't you? Silly girl. You've got so much else. Why squander yourself?'

They stared at each other. Her eyes were terribly frightened. But she kept silent. These were not the conditions to persuade her to talk. Perhaps he should have tried earlier. That time was past. For both of them.

'What can I do about you?' he asked thoughtfully. 'You may know what's going on. I doubt it. Gohar may have dropped hints but here a man's business is his private concern. If you know you probably accept his business as natural. After all, it's a wicked old world and you can say you can't change it and that the only thing is to make as much money as possible. All over the world women accept what men do, murder, blackmail, slavery, sodomy, exploitation, every crime and perversion. Why not you?'

'What are you talking about?'

'You. Another one who failed.'

Her eyes blazed at him. 'You must be mad!' she exclaimed.

He shuddered. 'Not that line, please,' he begged. 'It's a bit dusty . . . you telephoned Amer from the house just now. I heard the bell go as you rang off. So you must have told him I wanted to come here. The telephone was one error. There was another. You did not know I could drive yet you told me I could drive us here. You could have asked if I can drive, you should have asked. So Amer or someone told you I can drive. That means they knew I drove last night to that house which Amer has at Ma'an.'

Her eyes were nervous. 'Listen to me,' she said pleadingly.

'Wait,' he said. 'You told me several lies. The significant one was that they weren't back from their business trip. But the garage was full of new petrol fumes, and the air here is quite fresh. People used the garage recently, people have been here today.'

Now she was frightened. 'Please listen,' she begged.

'Shut up,' he said. 'I'm not complaining about how you lied. Most memorable. You'd be a lovely woman to make love with. But as a liar you're an amateur. Amer used you like he used Gohar and others. Right now, he and Mekki are somewhere near. They may have others with them. So you are in danger of being killed. I'd like to give you the benefit of the doubt. I hate seeing a woman go to waste.'

Every vestige of confidence had gone from her eyes while he spoke. Suddenly, without apparent change, she looked older, ten years older, her face just another battleground where age was the dreaded enemy working ceaselessly towards the day when her one hold over any man would be gone and she would be another woman surrounded by fresh unused girls in these lands of resignation to the rule of men.

After a slight hesitation she said: 'I don't want you to be killed.' Her voice sagged like an old sofa. 'They said you need not be harmed. He swore it. He said you could take me away. I have meant what I told you.'

'When did he say this to you?'

'This morning,' she said and her hands jerked up, reaching towards him. 'Let us go before it is too late. He promised.'

'What did he promise?'

'If I kept you away from them I could persuade you to take me away with you before Gohar returns because I want to go with you,' she said in a broken sort of voice. 'Wouldn't you like that?'

'I came here for something. He knows what it is. You may know. Where is it?'

Her eyes widened. 'I don't know what you're talking

about,' she said. 'By the Prophet, I swear it. They never told me their business. I want to go with you. They will come here soon if we do not go. Please . . .'

He shook his head. 'Stay close,' he said. 'If they get here while we're still here, well, they'll do their best to get rid of both of us in order to protect themselves. His promises to you today were lies. That I assure you.'

'He would not lie to me,' she said. 'I do know something of what they have done.'

'Exactly,' he said. 'Now, keep calm and keep quiet. A lot depends on you.'

As they went down the first line of tables he kept picking up dolls to test their weight. Anything approaching systematic search was impossible. It might also be useless. Amer and his associates had the advantage of several hours. He could only pray for luck.

Table after table defeated him. Allowing for the weight of his automatic, the dolls weighed equally in his hands. He began by picking them up singly, one in each hand. Then he hefted two in each hand and later clusters of three, the utmost he could manage satisfactorily. She did what he told her, retreated into traditional compliance in pursuit of her own purposes. Her face was expressionless and seemed to have thinned, the skin drawn over the bones, though that might be due to the lighting. Once or twice he caught sight of an uneasy flutter of her fingers. She said nothing.

Near the end of the third line of tables he stopped. He laid down the automatic and stood holding three dolls in either hand, six Virgins with downcast eyes and wearing long blue and white robes. Those in his left hand were slightly heavier. He was sure of it. He tested them singly. When he found the one which was heavier he went over it rapidly without finding outward cause for its additional weight. He stuffed it into the right-hand pocket of his jacket and picked up the automatic.

Halfway down the fifth row of tables he discovered

another heavier doll, a figure of Christ. His conviction increased. He jammed it into his pocket.

That was the last line of tables. At the bottom, the farthest point from the entrance, he stopped and glanced round. The obvious thing, the final proof or he was a moon-man, was still missing. Nofret Gohar stood silent and uncommunicative two paces away, eyes lowered, lips thin, her hands idle. He narrowed his lids to stare past the shine of lights at the ceiling. There was nothing visible up there. He turned to her.

'Where is the cellar?' he asked. 'I've been looking for it.'

She hesitated, then came forward quickly, her body against him though she kept her hands at her sides. 'Let us go,' she entreated urgently. 'We may still be able to escape from them.' Something of her previous confidence came back to her face and her voice regained its caressive tones. 'Take me with you. Anywhere. You shall never regret it. I want you, to be with you. Wherever you go and whatever you do, I will always be with you. You are the only man I have ever wanted in my life. Think of me——'

He shoved her back a pace. 'Be good,' he advised.

'I want to be your woman forever,' she said frantically.

He hunted through his own present tensions for sufficient patience. 'You don't want anything of the sort,' he told her gently. 'That's just what you feel at present, isn't it? You've felt like it over other men, God knows how many. Sometimes it's been just a man you've seen on a street.'

'No . . . no . . .'

'Yes. And you'll go on feeling the same things. You can't help it. You must keep possessing new men, or imagine you will possess them until someone easy comes along to kill your imagination. And you've got to keep on feeling new to yourself because of them. You must have men, unknown men, chance men, boys, anything male. It's a sickness. You can't help it.'

She raised a hand to strike him but it fell limp at her side. Her eyes beseeched his trust. 'It would be different with you,' she said pleadingly. 'I've never met a man like you. You're hard but you're gentle. You have so much. I would never betray you.'

'Not for two weeks maybe. Probably less. Then you would believe you knew everything and had had it. Honey, I know the symptoms. I was married to a woman like you. It wasn't her fault. She was beautiful too.'

'You could help me . . .'

'Where is the cellar?'

She hesitated.

'Come on,' he ordered harshly. 'Don't make me rough you up.'

'You wouldn't be cruel.'

'The cellar,' he said as they looked deep into each other's eyes. 'The cellar.'

She licked her lips. Her eyes turned aside under their heavy lids. 'They may be down there,' she said tightly.

'I doubt it. They wouldn't be such fools. It would complicate their situations. Why lock themselves in here and then hide? No, honey. Where is it?'

She bit her lip. Then she shrugged resignedly and turned, leading him to the farthest aisle, her shoulders down as they walked towards the tiny office. Halfway along she halted and pointed under the table. 'There,' she said dully.

He motioned her another two paces away and crouched down on his heels to examine it, keeping her legs and hands in close sight. The trapdoor, about three feet square, was made from four old strips of worn plank wood. Two trestles rested squarely on it. A carefully arranged mess of crumped tissue-paper had hidden it from his sight. It had an iron ring handle under another wad of tissue. The grooves along each side were noticeably free from dust. He straightened up.

'It's about forty feet from the office,' he said thoughtfully. 'Is there a light switch up here?'

'No.'

'Is there one down there?'

'No. They always use torches. Please don't go down——'

He looked at her. 'We,' he said. 'We're going down.'

That jarred her out of resignation. He saw the pupils of her eyes dilate. For some seconds her voice failed her. Eventually she spoke, the words tripping and colliding on her tongue, reverted to Arabic.

'By Allah, no!' she ejaculated violently. 'O man, I will not go down there, by Allah, no. There is nothing except rats, come from the village. As thou cherish the memory of thy mother and her milk, let me await thee here. By Abbas, I will not betray thee. Whatever thou desire of me later shall be thine and thy blood shall remember it joyously all thy days but spare me this thing. Whatever thou choose, we will do. For however little time we are together thou shalt be the sun and moon of my body but spare me this,' she begged, her lips shaking.

'Gently, woman,' he said. 'Why do you refuse to be with me down there?'

'No no. Man, everything else I will do and thou need never work again. Such places have terrified me since boys locked me in the vault under a ruined mosque when I was a small girl and I spent two days there half out of my mind. No! Anything else I will do, I swear by the loins of Fatimah.'

He would willingly have spared her, and himself, without reference to the daughter of the founder of the Muslim faith, but these circumstances left him without choice.

'There are rats everywhere,' he said, got his free hand under the trestle and lifted it and the long board off the trapdoor. Out of the corner of his eye he saw her poise as if to run for the entrance. He raised his gun. 'Don't force me to think solely of myself,' he warned her.

After a moment physical tension went out of her. She settled back on her heels, fear blurring her face like a mask of dust, her eyes staring, their pupils enormous. She began to mutter no no by Allah by Allah no by Abbas no, the words dribbling incoherently from her lips. He watched her carefully, then got hold of the iron ring and hauled up the trapdoor. A swift glance showed him a flight of worn wooden steps leading down into the darkness. He got his torch from his pocket.

'You first,' he said curtly.

'No no no no no no. . . .'

'We shall soon be out.'

'You know not what you do to me,' she muttered. 'I shall go mad . . . mad . . .'

He saw little point in telling her that he too was a ripe claustrophobic. Dark shut-in-places held little charm for him. Her naked terror hinted that both of them would finish by screaming up the flaming walls.

He waved the gun at her. 'You first,' he repeated. 'Amer and his friends got you into this. I'll get you out of it if I can. It depends on you.'

Her lips worked. 'You swear it?' she begged. 'You will not leave me down there alone?'

'I want both of us out of here.'

A little of the terror went from her eyes. She drew her breath quickly and took four nervous strides to the open trapdoor. He heard her moaning deep in her throat. She put her right foot on the first step and went quickly down into the darkness. He followed, flashing torchlight from side to side.

'Sixteen steps,' he said as he stepped off the bottom one onto an uneven stone floor. Around them were trestle tables similar to those above. On them were stacked boxes but he saw no sign of dolls. There were larger packing-cases against one wall. 'It's about fifty feet square,' he said thoughtfully.

He flashed torchlight across the ceiling. Its dusty surface failed to discover a light socket. Reason told him that was an advantage. A swarm of butterflies swarming around his stomach told him that reason was academic. They dreaded this sort of place. He turned to her. 'Where do they keep the dolls sent from China?' he asked. 'They must be here. I'm sure of it.'

She turned without speaking. He flashed light about to help her as she ran up between two lines of tables. Suddenly she stumbled and would have fallen if she had not caught hold of the nearest table. As she righted herself she glanced down. Instantly her hand covered her mouth in a vain attempt to check the scream which leapt from her throat. The sound seemed to drip down the walls around them.

He joined her. The torchlight played over a large man sprawled on his back at her feet. A man with crew-cut curly black hair and a jaw like a train buffer. His arms and legs were spread wide like a dancer doing a vast Nijinski jump. Except that he was horizontal. Whoever shot him had messed up his face. Another bullet had got him through the heart. His once neat dark suit and white shirt would never reach a secondhand-clothes stall in the *suq*.

She was moaning uncontrollably, her whole body shaking.

17

HE PUSHED her aside to step over and kneel to take a closer look.

It was rather unlovely. At a rough guess the other man had been flung aboard the big ship about eight hours ago. Climatic and other conditions might have affected rigor mortis; the cellar was noticeably cooler than the warehouse. One thing was certain. Muhammed Shvernik had embarked on his voyage elsewhere.

During embarkation a lot of blood had been lost. The bullet which got him in the face had torn a gaping hole above his upper lip directly under his nose. It had been fired from less than a foot away. His upper jaw was smashed. Jagged bone chips were caught by blood from his ruined mouth which had congealed on his chin and neck but nothing had dripped onto the floor. Dust smears and abrasions on his forehead suggested he had fallen on his face at some point prior to death. The other wound had caused blood to saturate a wide area of his clothes, but once again the floor beneath his left side was comparatively clean. Shvernik's pockets were empty. They and parts of his clothes had been sliced open methodically to get out whatever was concealed there. But he had got here. By means which would never be known, he had found a lead which brought him right into the organisation. And it had bumped him off the mortal coil. That suggested that he had been ignorant of what was happening. If true it also meant that Moscow was also ignorant. That was the conclusion though nowadays anything could happen.

He stood up flicking dust off his trousers. 'Where are they?' he asked.

She ignored the question. 'Who was he?' she got out through nerveless lips. Her voice was without positive tonal significance.

'Surely you met him?' he countered.

'I've never seen him till now.'

'Are you telling me they didn't pass him over for you to get to work on him?' he asked brutally. 'He was just the sort of man who would have pleased you. I'm sure of it.'

'No no . . .'

'His name was Muhammed Shvernik.'

'I never heard of him.'

'It's a big world. He may have used another name.'

'No no,' she kept moaning.

Their voices sank around them, each syllable withered directly it was spoken. The acoustics lent an eerie quality to what they said. He got an impression that she had better control of herself, traditionally distraught at the sight of violent death but also traditionally phlegmatic, aware that the bell tolled for everyone. He guessed that if her emotions were involved she would ululate for days. She tried to drag herself erect.

'You knew him,' she said like an accusation.

'We met,' he agreed. 'Where are they?'

She stepped over the body past him to where larger wooden packing-cases were stacked on one table. At his instruction she stood where he had clear sight of her. Then he took the loose lid off one case, laid the torch on the table with its beam directed at her and thrust his free hand into straw waste inside the case, searching around till he found three dolls and drew them out. At once a sense of vindication went through him. Each one was much heavier than the dolls laid out overhead.

As he shoved them into his pocket a voice above the open cellar door said: 'You will not take them away, Mr. Silk.' Although the cellar played tricks with timbre and sentence, the heavy gravel-churn voice was unmistakeable. While it spoke a ray of torchlight pinned Silk's face as if it was a butterfly. 'Put them back on the table,' Amer ordered in his weightiest tone.

Silk decided against heroic filibusters or appeals to reason. He flung himself at the woman. The force of their spring sent them sprawling to the floor. Bullets whined over where they had stood. The noise slapped around the cellar and dribbled away. When his hearing oozed back he heard Amer raving furiously at Mekki. Beneath him the woman whimpered ceaselessly. He told her to shut up. She disregarded his instructions so he slapped her. Though his hand missed her face his fingers struck her jaw.

As quietness returned he heard Amer ask if he could hear. The torchlight searched around for them like a fumbling hand. He turned his head aside. 'I hear you,' he said breathlessly.

'Put down your gun and come up where I can see you. It is your only chance. If you refuse both of you will be killed.'

The woman moaned. 'I did what you told me,' she kept saying thickly and struggled to release herself.

He shoved her back on the floor. 'Shut up,' he snarled. 'Do you think he'll spare you? He'll kill you like a fly. He'll get another woman, younger, much younger. Shut up, you fool.'

'Can you hear me?' the voice churned.

'Hardly.'

'Either let her go or let her get up.'

He laughed incredulously. 'Don't be idiotic,' he called back, put his hand on her neck and pressed down on it. 'You've got a lot of money down here. Come down and save it. Your employers won't like this. You've ruined their plans. They'll get rid of you.'

'Let her go.'

'So you can kill her and say I did it? This afternoon she did what you told her to do but I'm keeping her here. Did you tell her you killed her husband yesterday? Did you?'

In the pause which followed he relaxed his pressure on her throat. She lay still, breathing heavily. Then the voice grated: 'Son of filth, you killed him because you lust to possess her.'

He shook her. 'Do you hear?' he asked. 'Listen to him, listen to him, listen.' He raised his voice. 'You disease come from the bowels of pigs, I cannot hear you. What did you say?'

'I say you killed him to possess her. She is a sick whore.'

'Did you hear?' he whispered hopelessly, certain she was incapable of coherent thought. 'Now do you realise why I told you to help me? He'll kill you if he gets the chance.' He raised his voice. 'Yes yes yes, I hear you. You're a fool, an amateur. A camel could do your work better. Your employers will get rid of you. You think you're safe because you know who they are and can tell others. You're wrong. They're going to kill you because you're clumsy. Shall I tell you why? You couldn't even run me down with your car the other evening. You can't even conceal your true activity.'

He talked on, forcing a hearing during these few seconds while Amer switched from whatever plan he had devised as he followed them into the warehouse to a makeshift plan to deal with this situation. It might be his last chance to confuse that gross fixer up there. It was certainly his last opportunity to persuade her to think. She had ceased to struggle. That meant nothing. Sooner or later everyone had to have a rest, physically and mentally, from whatever storm possessed them. He feared lest she might writhe clear at the instant when he least expected it.

Other concerns crowded his mind. Half of his body kept her on her back and his free hand was on her neck ready to prevent her from calling out. He kept shifting his head, trying to pitch his voice from various angles to prevent them from pin-pointing where she and he lay.

Their torchlight hunted around. There were two beams.

They came close but were stopped by the tables. On the table above his feet his torch lay where he had put it down. It threw its ray across the cellar but it was quartered by boxes in its path. It gave the opposition little help but it might betray him if in wriggling round his legs brought the table down on them. Yet somehow before fast dwindling time ran out he must get it and switch off its light.

He stopped calling to the distant man to draw breath. Although she lay inert like someone who had fainted, he saw her eyes twitching from side to side under their long lids. 'For God's sake keep quiet,' he whispered, 'it's our one chance.' He wondered how many men were up there.

The distant voice grated at him. 'You are wasting your energy, Silk,' it said.

'Wrong again.'

'You are alone. You would be wiser to agree to what I tell you.'

'Do you really think I would come here without taking precautions?'

'There is nobody outside.'

His heart sank.

He laughed. 'Ah?' he jeered. 'You go on believing that if you want to. I told you, you're an amateur. You followed me and they have followed you.'

While they shouted at each other, swopping the Arabic insults which were part of a time-honoured formula to debase one's enemy, he began to shift his body round. It was tricky. He was getting a bit rusty for these gymnastics after a night like last night. They should be done by an agile youth who could walk on his thumbs with his legs round his neck. He paused to draw breath, aware of hurtable joints. He renewed his activity, extricating his legs from those of a trestle. There were seconds when he had to take risks on her foolhardy hope of saving the flesh she enjoyed.

Somehow he managed it. Neither of the searching torches caught him. She was ominously still, breathing evenly.

Miraculously he shifted round to face the stairs without bringing the table down on them. He raised his gun hand cautiously, freezing it while torchlight prowled near. As it flickered away his knuckles touched the edge of the table. He eased them along to near the place where he thought his torch was lying.

'Give in, Silk. You will not leave here unless I allow it. You can take that she-camel with you if you want her. Give in.'

He laughed again. 'You're absurd,' he called back. 'You're making it worse for yourself. Be sensible. Call off those thugs. If you give yourself up I'll help you. You're at the end of the road, Amer. If you don't give in now your employers will kill you.'

Suddenly several things happened. He had reached his gun-arm up and over the table at the back of the torch and felt its metal edge come against the side of his hand, put his hand on it and pressed his wrist down in an effort to drag it back towards the edge of the table without changing the direction of its beam. The amount of pressure he had to use made the ray wobble. Instantly the distant torches flicked their light towards it. He steadied his wrist on the torch and squeezed the trigger. His gun and one of those high up on the staircase fired simultaneously. He jerked his wrist back. The torch cartwheeled slowly, its light swinging over and going out as it struck the floor near him. At the same instant the woman heaved herself up. He grabbed her down the waist in a rugger tackle and yanked her back. The other gun fired twice while she fought to free herself. She really was a strongly built girl. He heard the distant voice order Mekki to go down and kill them. It said they would wait for him. Then there was only one torch shining.

He heard footsteps patter down the steps. The torch went off. He thrust the struggling woman down on her back and waited. A moment later the other torch flashed on. It was several feet over on the right of the bottom of the steps. It switched off immediately. The whole cellar went completely black. Without joy he realised that the trapdoor had been shut. His hordes of butterfles multiplied fantastically.

A phenomenal silence settled down on them. Within yards of the woman and himself the other man breathed softly as a cat, waiting for something to betray their location.

Silk lifted his head slowly. He drew his legs under him, preparatory to rising. Accidentally his left leg bumped against his torch and it rolled away. As he groped for it the woman jerked away screaming terror into the stillness. A split second later his hand found the torch lying against her naked warm thigh and realised she must have thought it was a rat. Her screams went on.

Recklessly, the other torch was searching for them. Its light went far over on their right in an attempt to get behind them. The reverberations of two shots slapped his ears like slamming doors. One ploughed into wood and rocked the long table over their heads. The second whipped boxes and dolls onto the floor on their left. At once the torch went out. She continued to scream; God alone knew where she found the breath or the energy but she found them. He did the only thing possible. His hand searched up over her body till it reached her face. Then his fist hit her jaw hard enough to break the high wail of fear though he dared not risk knocking her out. An illusion of quietness returned. Through the singing in his ears he heard her whimpering.

He lay still wondering what the hell he could do. There was precious little opportunity to manœuvre in these conditions where every stir of a limb was fraught with hazards.

Gradually, quarter-inch by quarter-inch, he eased back across the floor, unsure of what he should do yet knowing he should try to reach the other wall before the man slid between it and them. His every effort was hampered by the half-unconscious woman.

He heard nothing over on his right, no sound of breathing which could guide or warn.

At length he paused to get his breath and thumbed up

the switch of his torch. His fears proved correct. The bulb had gone, probably when it hit the floor. He sniffed the air. Some new but intangible element mingled elusively with the general staleness and smell of old dirt.

He eased back, stopped directly his outstretched feet met an obstacle and fumbled them at it till he obtained a belief that it was a trestle leg. He slid his left arm under her thighs and drew her after him. She was as cooperative as a sack of potatoes. He went on, hauling her slowly. His right forearm was raised and his gun ready for what might prove to be the last emergency.

As the other light snapped on he went still. It had shifted again. Unless it was a trick of place or nerves, it seemed closer. He started to crawl back on his belly like a blind worm, drawing her soft resistless weight with him.

Minutes or ages later, while he was wondering if the wall had receded by some hellish freak or if he had lost his way, the torch came on again. It was low on the floor, its beam directed to where they had lain at first. He had a clear sight of its point of origin free from intervening obstructions. It turned towards them. He steadied his gun hand and fired slightly to its right. There was a sharp cry. He fired again. When the din faded he heard a dribbling moan. It went silent. The light stayed on. Then it dipped sideways across the floor towards the flight of stairs.

He got up and blundered wildly across the cellar, knocking over the end of one table in his haste, hearing boxes and dolls slide onto the floor, never losing sight of the motionless ray of light, his ears alert for any warning sound. There was none. When he got to the torch and turned its light down he saw that the man who lay on his side on the floor would never make another sound. In these circumstances it was a fluke shot which killed Mekki though both had got him. One had entered his head above his left ear. The other had ripped the deltoid muscles of his shoulder. He had gone aboard the big ship as fast as any other traveller.

Silk crouched down on his heels to search the dead man. 'Oh, shut up,' he snarled as the woman began to moan noisily again. He coughed drily, his throat irritated by the unplaceable smell mixing with the odours of staleness and dirt.

He discovered that the new passenger had carried a fair-sized arsenal in the hope of remaining at this port whilst helping others to embark. Beside him lay a Czech imitation of a Smith & Wesson .45. One pocket contained a snub-nosed Japanese automatic. Another had the latest small Beretta, just the weapon for single businesswomen working late at the office. He had a sheath knife strapped to his left arm and another for throwing, fastened under his right knee like a skean dhu. Seemingly he had felt insecure among his fellow inhabitants of these lands.

Silk coughed again. There were papers in the dead Mekki's pockets. He stuffed them into his own pockets among dolls and other bric-à-brac.

There was nothing else of interest. At length he stood up, coughing, and stumbled back to the moaning woman. He switched torchlight onto the table and cleared a space. Then he hauled her up and put her into a sitting position. He supported her against his chest. Without his aid she would have sprawled down onto the floor again.

Unfortunately for both of them, she was in poor shape. Her coordination had gone. She was completely nerveless, unable to make an independent action to help him, beyond speech. Her head had fallen forward on her neck, tangled hair loose over her shoulders. But her nerves were the main sufferers. Her bruises were superficial. Her clothes were only soiled.

He said something meaningless and coughed wretchedly.

Suddenly a new idea occurred to him. He swung the torchlight towards the trapdoor. Its glow confirmed his fear. Thin coils of smoke sidled down between the planks and spread like fog into the cellar.

He ran round the table to the stairs and up them to start

shoving at the trapdoor. Smoke crept around his face like eels. His efforts were unavailing. The trapdoor did not budge an inch. He strained and sweated, exerting the maximum strength he could in this position, till another fiercer bout of coughing forced him back down the stairs. After a pause he went up them and tried again. The trapdoor remained solidly in position. Four men might have done it. Four big men who chewed nails for breakfast.

He went back to the woman. Fortunately, she was without realisation of what had happened. She lay crumpled on the table, her legs dangling over the edge. He fought down another bout of coughing. A flash of torchlight showed that the smoke was thickening. He tried to think coherently. He had never done his clearest thinking while boxed up inside a cell while claustrophobia rampaged through his nerves. Unsurely he went over to the farthest corner. He switched torchlight around. The ceiling was vanishing above a hateful cloud.

He wiped sweat off his forehead and licked his lips. 'I don't know if you are receiving me,' he said, speaking distinctly. 'If you are, listen to what comes after the next few sentences. They have set the warehouse on fire and she and I are trapped in the cellar. I have tried to raise the trapdoor but they've stacked things on it so'—he coughed—'we may be in for an exit by suffocation . . . about Shvernik. Either they caught him after they failed to run me down or he got to one of their houses and was caught. He wasn't killed here.'

'Who are you talking to?' the woman asked in a quavery voice.

'Friends,' he said, and went on: 'Listen carefully. They may hope to destroy the evidence here by this fire. Their plan is clear but I lack factual evidence for most points.' He coughed for some moments. 'Now listen. The first names on their list of victims were either ex-members of the gang who got cold feet or people who refused to assist it. Their real targets'—he coughed again—'are later names, shaikhs or relatives of . . . shaikhs and rulers along the Persian Gulf, rulers of the oil states. They intend to kill or . . . terrorise them into . . . submission in order to prevent oil from going to the West. To do this they have . . . recruited an organisation which uses people who will kill in order to get narcotics. My guess is their killers are all addicts. They borrowed this idea from the . . . Assassins. The drug . . . is opium. It's smuggled here in dolls, imported from China, chiefly, I suspect, those wearing Yunnan regional costume. . . . Yunnan is the main opium producing region. They also supply other addicts who . . . sell it. This is a four-pronged bid to . . . undermine Russian influence . . . get oil which Russia has cut off from China . . . deprive Europe of its main oil supplies . . . and raise . . . money through selling opium. I'm pretty . . . sure part . . . part of the stuff goes to Europe and America, through places like Greece . . . and . . . Italy . . .' He broke off, trying to ignore the smoke feathers sliding down his throat. 'I hope you've heard me,' he got out breathlessly. 'There may be factual . . . evidence . . . somewhere.'

'Why do you keep talking?' the woman asked in Arabic and torchlight showed her stumbling towards him, her hands feeling along the tables. 'Man, what has happened? Why is there so much dust? Can we go now?'

'Soon.'

'Come with me,' she pleaded in a crooning voice, 'we will be alone there.' She coughed. 'I want to be against you and feel your hands on me. Your hands are fine manly hands. It shall be good for you.' She laughed and coughed. Her hands came from the darkness to touch his face. 'O man, you shall find cause to come back to me.' Her fingers searched over his cheeks and lips. She tried to put her hands round him. 'Man, I am the one woman whose loving you shall never forget,' she muttered and laughed dreamily. 'Hold me, touch me, eh! *sahlim ideeq . . . Allah yitaw'wil umrqum*—may God lengthen thy life.'

He steadied her with his arm. It was about all he could

do for her. At present she was a goof. From the hour of her visit to his hotel room, when she let slip that bit of information which gave him a theory, he had been pretty sure she was a nymph. Now a succession of strains had taken control of her. She had been hit hard, too hard, and the hitting had gone on inside her mind while she lay on the floor till everything had become tangled, and her mind had retreated into delusions which gave her a form of quietness. The touch of his hand on her hair brought murmurs of pleasure from her. She was oblivious to their plight. They might have been young lovers alone on a flower-spangled hill graced by spring sunlight. They might have been the last man and woman alive, or the first, rejoicing in their uniqueness. Poor unfortunate woman.

He coughed miserably and spat phlegm. 'If you heard that you know I've a slight problem down here,' he said breathlessly. 'Now I'm going to try to get out of here. If I fail you'll find their papers stuck under the bath at my hotel. Use them. I'll take care of her if it——'

He retched vilely, hawking up mouthfuls of saliva. He wished dully that there was water so he could drench his handkerchief or her stockings to protect their mouths and nostrils. As the bout of coughing eased he was sweating. Then he lifted his head to listen.

Abruptly he hauled her forward towards the stairs. In the last few minutes the smoke had thickened noticeably. It deflected light from the torch or absorbed it like a cloud absorbed sunlight. Amid bouts of coughing he heard the heavy dragging overhead which had attracted his attention. Once he nearly lost his path to the stairs. He had to half carry her. She was near collapse, her legs unable to support her. His eyes streamed. His lungs were bags of smoke.

Somehow he got her to the foot of the stairs. Both of them were retching now. He dragged her up, driven on by a sort of madness. At the top, in the thickest smoke, he met his worst difficulty, turning round while shifting her heavy weight into his other arm. Again, somehow, he succeeded. Another bout of retching like insanity shook him from head to foot. He felt his senses drifting. He wobbled unsteadily and nearly fell full length down the stairs. Then he was bent double, unbreathing, his back jammed up against the trapdoor. His legs trembled under the strain of effort.

At his first heave the door rose about a quarter of an inch and then flapped down on him. At the second effort he might have been trying to push over the Rock of Gibraltar with his little fingers. Feeling sick, he slackened the pressure, got another hold on the woman and shifted his feet. At this attempt he did get the trapdoor up slightly, maybe an inch. His back felt as if it was about to snap under the weight. Then the door went up another inch and then another. Without warning it had gone. He swayed unsteadily.

Through the clouds of smoke swirling down a thin hand clutched his shoulder. He tightened his grasp on the woman's waist. Awkwardly, weakly, coughing hopelessly, he backed up into the burning warehouse. Once again he shoved his arm farther round the woman's waist and she almost caused both of them to fall back into the cellar.

The next phase was a chaotic blur. Five minutes or a hundred years later the three of them lay on the ground outside watched by an excited small crowd. As his eyes peered through the wetness he caught sight of the girl lying face down coughing. She was covered in grime and specks of burnt paper. Her short-clipped hair was like a dirty dishcloth. He knew that she could not have heard his lengthy explanation over the bug. Part of her clothes were charred from flames which licked round her while she dragged trestles off the trapdoor. Even so, she was better off than the woman on the other side of him. She was unconscious.

He got to his knees and turned and saw that the warehouse was blazing. Two village men ran up with pitchers of water. He took one and sipped it gratefully. Nothing had ever tasted so good. 'Allah reward thee, brother,' he said and coughed. He took another sip.

The girl sat up blinking at him from bloodshot eyes. 'I thought . . .' she said.

'So did I . . . here, drink some of this.'

Their efforts to revive the woman were unavailing till he threw water into her face. Then she moaned and her body turned onto her side.

'Help me,' he said.

They got her up supporting her between them and dragged her to the car which had brought the girl. He got them into the back and settled himself into the driving-seat. His eyes kept blurring and spasms of renewed coughing racked him. But there was an absence of bullets though he did not trust the group of people. Among them there must be at least one who would rush to the nearest telephone to pass on the information. He put the car in gear and drove widely round on the road heading towards Jerusalem.

On the drive back he got back a measure of energy though he did everything automatically. At the approach to the city he told the girl that she must take the woman to her hotel room because he needed the car. She heard him without speaking.

Directly he had dropped them he drove on, circling back through the evening traffic to the suburb which contained Hamadan Road. He pulled up a short distance from the house. Then he switched on the receiving-box on the seat beside him. At first he had to turn it to gain contact with the bug which he had pinned inside the angel. Voices came to him. One was the gravel-grate issuing frantic orders and talking carelessly, far too carelessly. He wondered if one of the others belonged to Sabri. He relaxed on the seat, still sweating, the evening heat close about him, listening to what the men said as they got ready to run.

He coughed, wishing he had brought a pen and note-book. His memory was a see-saw between present and recent past.

It took nearly an hour. He was still sitting there when their car drove past him. After some moments he wiped his face. Then he put the car in gear.

He felt a bit achy as he went back to the hotel and up to his room. And as he opened the door he saw Rand sitting on the bed. Rand was like something out of a West End catalogue in his neat dark grey suit, his immaculate white shirt with its faultless cuffs, a discreet tie which would have given Queen Victoria a thrill of pleasure, his gleaming black shoes, his beautifully done, faintly reddish hair-do.

Rand raised his head. 'Hello, old man,' he said cheerfully and stood up, coming forward with an outstretched hand and flashing teeth. 'How are you, old boy? I've come to help you. Don't fret. Everything will be fine, under control. I say, have you had a fall? You look a bit dusty.'

Silk hitched up a smile. 'Ah,' he said and swallowed bile. 'Hello hello. Nice to see you. You're just in time.'

18

IT WAS several months later. Cairo slid towards a pleasant winter. Every sign suggested it might be more temperate than usual. Dragomen and fellahin, those infallible experts of climatic conditions, prophesied it confidently. That presaged good tourist business. Rumour had it that lissom young women were limbering up by rolling their bellies in readiness to entertain fat old men with frosty loins at hush-hush parties where devotees of the churning navel still cheated the government ban on traditional amusements.

Visitors already mingled with the city's rapidly rising population. There were businessmen from across the Atlantic. There were non-aligned businessmen from nearby. There were orange-squash businessmen from parts of Asia. There were visiting politicians.

The latter were from every Muslim country, most of them familiar with the noise and emotional effervescence and flowering pride encountered here. Ostensibly they were here to further Arab unity but this always meant their own careers. Every hour they speechified about it and smiled ruthlessly through television interviews. Quite a number of them were anxious to find out which of their Arab brothers were arranging to assassinate them, plotting their removal by accident or bullet or hanging or poison to precipitate rebellion or military coup called popular uprising, and each one was budgeting extra amounts to outwit their enemies by murdering them first. It was the ancient Arab game of kiss and kill; nobody believed in the endless toothy friendliness but everybody observed the conventions. They were here. Ambitious officers with secret alliances and well-greased palms. Oil shaikhs. Political nonentities with the warm licking tongue. Men who pursued old family feuds.

The chessboard was full.

Silk was also there. For once he was idle. It was good to relax. Given its fair chance, modern Cairo was a good city for relaxation. Out of the blue Swann had decided that he should have a rest while the changeover confusion of politicians at Westminster sorted itself out. Amazed, he had taken advantage of the offer without giving Swann a chance to withdraw it; there were limits to the extent of human consideration shown by Swann, who knew when he had a sucker on the pay-roll. He had concluded his other assignment and the latest developments going on through the area were still in their preliminary stages.

So he lolled on cushions and carpets in the comfortable living-room of the houseboat which his companion had rented from an Egyptian film actress who was filming in India for several weeks.

Through the windows he could see the lights of apartment blocks rising above trees flanking this western shore of the Nile. The atmosphere was pleasant. He felt almost benign. His companion and he had enjoyed an excellent dinner at a small restaurant which provided first-rate French cuisine on the assumption that its clientele was composed of new oil multimillionaires eager to spread the information around town. Still, he did owe her a good meal. Only one other woman had undertaken personal risks on the extraordinary assumption that his corporal entity was worth saving. To his further astonishment she had actually wanted to see him again, had gone to the lengths of finding out where he was and sent an invitation to visit her here if he came this way while she was here. It seemed logical to combine these separate factors tidily.

He leafed through a copy of the *New Yorker* which she had left beside him while she went to brew coffee. He saw that she was also halfway through one of the more reliable biographies of Christopher Marlowe. As he read what was showing in New York she brought in a tray laden with a worthwhile pot of coffee, cups like those you had at home, and glasses flanking a bottle of *araq*.

'Stay where you are,' she ordered at his effort to get up. 'I can manage.'

He still thought the claim pretty impossible. She just didn't look like it. Since leaving him a short while ago she had changed into black slacks and a black blouse. They enhanced her physical fragility, the thin neck, those childish wrists and hands. She looked even more like a fifteen-year-old girl who should be wrestling with her sums. Her short black hair curled over her neat head like leaves. Gold slippers were on her small feet. They provided the one touch of colour. On her it was just right.

She knelt down to place the tray between them and then poured out *araq* and black coffee. Her face was serious as she performed each task. Then she seated herself on the adjoining cushions with her legs curled under her.

She tasted the coffee speculatively. 'I've had worse,' she said. 'Did you ever hear what happened to him?'

He knew whom she meant. 'Oh, yes,' he said and tried the *araq*. 'Mmmm, pretty good. I'll send you to market again. Yes, I heard. We newspapermen have our methods and they are good enough to get on the trail of clumsy idiots like Amer. Directly he cleared out of the house he went to Amman. Two days later he turned up in Basra. Then he went to Sharjah and vanished. The next thing was that my—what did you call it? unimportant?—my unimportant newsagency sold the story to a world market. We had it in nearly three hundred papers ahead of magazine articles. We had enough information on other cells, not all of them but the important one. That was because he talked at the house while I was listening. So, end of the Prophet organisation. Two weeks later he was found stabbed to death outside Sharjah. That was what happened to him.' He had another drink. 'I hear they have another organisation going. Without religion. A sort of Murder Incorporated. How about Sabri? Did you ever hear of him? We couldn't trace him.'

She shook her head. 'I never heard of him,' she said. 'Your theory about him may have been right.'

'There was evidence . . . why did the Chinese visit him?'

She stared at him thoughtfully. 'I wonder,' she said. ' Sabri was very resourceful.'

'That too, like patriotism, is not enough.'

'Think of the men who get into jams and get out whole. You did.'

'There is always some dark alley next year. Be warned, child, be warned. You're wasting your abilities . . . oh, incidentally, those chaps came from ports along the Persian Gulf, another proof of how the scheming riff-raff from round here consistently abuse the hospitality of Jordan, as they have for years and years . . . where was I? Oh yes, that episode was a bit rough-and-tumble. Some affairs are. Others are complicated. Some begin complicated but fall apart. Whichever it might be, I think a girl like you can find better outlets for her abilities.'

'Must you be so damn fatherly?' she snarled.

'Is that how I sound? Well well well well well well.'

She stared at him. 'I'm going home next month,' she said.

'Good.'

She flushed. 'Killing doesn't appeal to me,' she said and reached for his glass. 'I took care of her. What does it taste like?'

'Try it,' he told her. 'What about her?'

She sniffed cautiously over the rim of the glass. 'It smells odd,' she said. 'She'll soon be as right as she wants to be. I did what you said, drove her to the hospital at Beirut where they put her under sedation. Later she talked to me. It was what we suspected. I saw her three weeks ago. She's enjoying herself. The hospital is stuffed with handsome doctors. She mentioned him but she kept talking about you. I told her I didn't know where you were.'

He raised his brows. 'Spoilsport,' he commented. 'I bet it ruined her day. Still, she'll enjoy the change. And changes we are having everywhere, aren't we? You know, I'm going to miss Khrushchov and his delightful wife. Well, go on, try it,' he suggested.

She let a little liquor run into her mouth, then wrinkled her nose. 'Golly!' she said and sneezed.

'Others feel as if you've swallowed a flame-thrower.'

'It surely is an acquired taste.'

She gave him back the glass and poured a thimbleful into the other glass and put down the bottle.

He talked brightly about other changes which had taken place.

After a moment she interrupted. 'Well, here we are,' she said. 'Aren't we?'

'I should say we were. Eeyop. Here we are.'

Her eyes smiled. 'You've read Dorothy Parker,' she said.

'You bet your sweet life I have.'

She picked up her glass and sniffed at it warily and lowered it. Her hands did everything gracefully. She stretched out her legs in front of her like a boy while she looked down at the glass. Her hair was in a fine old state. 'Dorian . . .' she said.

'Mmmm?'

'Were you ever in love?'

He gazed blankly at her lowered head. Then he decided it was a legitimate question, honestly put, without risk. 'Long ago and far away,' he said. 'She's better off wherever she is. I'm not the lovable type. This job is another complication. It stops a woman from flipping a coin to decide if she can get resigned to the other usual monotonies. Who'll care in fifty years? What about you?'

She nodded briefly and her lips held that small smile which he had not forgotten. 'He was married,' she said. 'Dorian, I don't do that to another woman, even one without children.'

'Good for you,' he said. 'About drinking.'

'Yes?'

'There are two schools of thought. Stay clear or be in command so it can't frighten you.'

'You subscribe to the second attitude,' she said like a serious child.

'It seems logical. I keep off it when I'm at work on a story.'

'Are you at work now?'

'You tell me.'

'Help yourself.'

'I'll get around to it.'

Abruptly she raised her glass and swallowed her drink at a gulp and sneezed again. Then she drew air down her throat. 'It's a good thing we're not drinking at a club,' she said. 'My legs would go peculiar.'

'I could carry you.'

She put down her glass. 'Yes,' she said absently. After a pause she turned her head towards him and raised her eyes. 'Let's have another drink,' she said but did not attempt to fill their glasses. As they looked at each other her lips regained the full softness which he had seen once before and now it was more than a sort of alchemy. It was all sorts of things. She heeled off her shoes. 'You'll find hotels here very expensive,' she said practically, 'more expensive than a trip to the moon or somewhere quieter.'

'I'm only here for a few days.'

'So am I.' Did I tell you you're very *zoftig?*'

Her hands took hold of the one he held out to her. 'What sort of proper things do you think I can find to do?' she asked, and flushed under his gaze.

Author's Note

The transliteration of Arabic into English causes continuous problems. There are few generally accepted renditions and regional variations increase the overall problem. Many Britons still use the transliterations given by Charles Doughty in his *Arabia Deserta*, published in 1888. Later writers have given other spellings of speech sounds made by the 28 letters of the Arabic alphabet. Thus, the Arabic for bazaar used to be given as *souk*; others give it as *souq*; the nearest rendition to sound is *suq*. Again, the transliteration for one who accepts the faith of Islam, 'submission' to the Will of God, has been given as Moslem, 'Mohammedan' or follower of Mahomet (the founder of the faith whose name has been given as Mohammed, Mehemet, Mohamed, and Muhammed), and Muslim (Mu'slim). 'The Koran'—the Islamic Bible—is more accurately given as Al-Quran or the Qu'ran. The most difficult Arabic letter sound is that given originally in English as k; its actual sound is nearer to q. Moreover, certain Arabic words, like others in other languages, have gained a different meaning outside their own language. One is *hashish* (ha'shish) which means fodder whereas Western languages have absorbed it as the name of hemp used as a narcotic.

The problems facing Western writers trying to record the quality of spoken Arabic are endless. Few Arabs speak classical Arabic—it is as remote as is Latin—but the colloquial tongue, full of regional variations, often appears unreal in transliteration despite its robustness and salty humour. Those who have read the fine novels of Naguib Mahfouz and Abdul Sharkawi, the Egyptian writers, will have noted their individual solutions.

I have always given transliterations into English as they have struck my ear. In this they follow the Arabic speech sounds which I learned from the late St. John Philby, an acquaintance of many years, adviser of the late Ibn Saud (E'bn Sou'ud), and one of the greatest authorities on the Arab and the Arab complex. I was extremely fortunate to have him as my original tutor into one of the most fascinating races of men.

SIMON HARVESTER